Tassie and the BLACK BARON

CLARE LITTLEJOHN

Tassie
and the
BLACK
BARON

Katie Roy

EGMONT

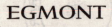

EGMONT
We bring stories to life

First published in Great Britain 2010
by Egmont UK Limited
239 Kensington High Street
London W8 6SA

Text copyright © 2010 Katie Roy
Cover illustration © 2010 Chris Mould
Cover design by Tom Hartley

The moral rights of the author have been asserted

ISBN 978 1 4052 4231 8

3 5 7 9 10 8 6 4 2

A CIP catalogue record for this title is available from the
British Library

Typeset by Avon DataSet Ltd, Bidford on Avon, Warwickshire
Printed and bound in Great Britain by the CPI Group

For Kieran and Jamie

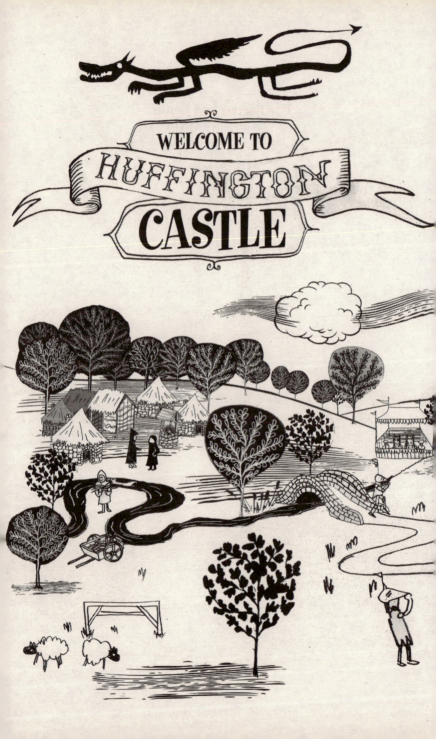

WELCOME TO HUFFINGTON CASTLE

Chapter 1

'Yaaay!' sang out Tassie, as the car sped past the entrance to the castle for the third time.

'They moved the sign!' shouted her dad angrily, looking for a place to do a hand-brake turn. 'Can you believe it . . . ? They moved the . . .'

'Well, *I* saw it, George,' said her mother, hanging on to her seat grimly.

'We saw it first!' squeaked the Twins, in the middle row.

'And we're goin' the wrong way down a one-way street!' cried Tassie happily, from the back.

Many of Tassie's friends suffered from a slightly embarrassing parent, but only Tassie could boast an entire family that made her toes curl. And she'd rather stay in the car than arrive at Huffington with them. The castle was to be the latest in a long line of family expeditions to what her mum called 'Places of Interest'. Usually they weren't, and the most fascinating thing about them was how quickly the Ripleys were told to leave.

Tassie also didn't want to stop because she was just about to give the Twins, Sam and Lil, a big dose of their own diabolical medicine. Quietly, she loosened her seatbelt, and leant forward. She was just about to stick one of Sam's gelled hair spikes and a long, white ribbon of Wrigley's Spearmint together for all eternity, when there was a sudden, furious howl of 'IMBECILE!' from her dad at the wheel, and she was hurled violently sideways. Through the rear window she snatched a glimpse of a gawping, terrified man on a zebra crossing, before the car skewed its way up the curb, around a large cherry tree in someone's garden, and then back on to the road.

'For goodness' sake!' shouted Tassie's dad crossly at the rear-view mirror. 'Why can't people just look where they're going?'

Her dad subsided into low-level growling and the

family breathed again. This close encounter with a petrified passer-by was nothing new on a Ripley family day out, but this time it had put Tassie in an uncomfortable spot. Sharing her kingdom of the rear seats was a large and ancient lady who seemed to be made up mostly of floral hat and skirt, with a lacy blouse sandwiched firmly in between. She clung to a carved wooden cane, decorated in stickers from a hundred different countries, and around her floated the peculiar smell of boiled cabbage. This peculiar vision was one of her mother's 'strays' – the only thing more likely than the Twins to ruin a day trip – and now the unbelted Tassie had been hurled right across the old girl's lap. Suddenly introductions had become necessary.

'Um. Hi,' said Tassie, gazing up at an impressive series of chins. 'I'm Tassie.'

'I know,' said the old lady. 'Here, I rescued your chewing gum. You dropped it . . . can't waste that, can we?' She winked, and they both turned slowly towards the unsuspecting Sam . . .

'Do you really live just next door?' Tassie asked with interest a few minutes later, after studying her partner in crime. The only thing that made her own house remarkable, in a very unremarkable street, was the tumbledown mess next door. Tassie had been 'borrowing' apples from the overgrown garden ever since she was big enough to fall out of a tree, and she'd never dreamt anyone actually lived there!

The old lady looked at her. Her blue eyes were very bright, but her skin was mostly heading south. Her blouse was crisp and clean, though frayed around the collar, and she wore the sort of skirt that fits neatly under the armpits. Finally, she was wading her way through a bag of sweets the size of a potato sack.

'Oh yes,' she said with a chocolatey smile, 'I've watched you all grow up. Remember when you buried the Twins' trumpet in the compost heap? Or when you used to sneak over the fence and steal my apples?'

Tassie slumped back, her mouth open. 'Spooky,' she

breathed. She wondered if the old lady had watched her experiments in the garden, eating ants, worms and beetles for no reason except that no one had actually told her not to. But she wasn't too bothered. After all, that was years ago. Well, about two years ago.

Within minutes, Tassie and the old girl were good friends. With typical Tassie bluntness, she asked how old her companion was. Tassie would have guessed somewhere in the mid hundreds.

'How old do you reckon?' asked the old lady. 'Well, actually,' she went quickly on as Tassie opened her mouth to give an unnecessarily honest reply, 'I do have to say I'm knocking on a bit.'

'Really?' said Tassie, interested. 'And what bit are you knockin' on?'

'Difficult to pin it down after all this time. Let's just say . . . I'm practically everyone's grandma.'

So Gramma she quickly became. Their conversation was then interrupted by a flurry of excitement in the front as, by sheer good luck, Huffington Castle appeared on the hill before them. Even when the handbrake had been applied, and the passengers spilt out into the car park, Mr Ripley was a still a deep shade of purple. No one took any notice. Sam and Lil had already found the ice cream van and were giving the unfortunate seller their famous 'angel-twin/devil-twin' routine, until the poor man bribed them with two Giganta-Cones to go away. Tassie was helping Gramma to unload herself by taking hold of her stick and yanking her out of the car like a well-fitting cork from a bottle, while Mrs Ripley encouraged her with words like 'Gently dear' and 'Oh I knew she was going to fall over'.

Gramma wheezed a bit, but didn't seem to mind. She just dusted herself down, while Mr Ripley went off to buy tickets at the drawbridge, and the Twins ran back with their sticky prizes.

'Hey Sam, let's see if we can swallow a whole cone without chewing!' said Lil to her brother. 'One, two, three, GO!' And she watched with interest as his cone vanished and ice cream splatted across his clothes. 'We' tended to mean 'you' in these cases, Tassie knew.

Sam didn't mind. He would have done it first if he'd thought of it.

'Aagh!' panted Sam. 'My brain's frozen!'

Huffington Castle must have been very grand in its day, thought Tassie. She climbed up a steep grassy slope to stand under its walls, and strained her neck back to look up at the battered battlements. Far above she could see jet-black rooks, throwing themselves off the stonework, and soaring across the open countryside beyond. She wished she could do that! It must be fabulous to swoop up and down in the warm summer air. She wondered if rooks were ever afraid of heights, and imagined a gang of them cawing to each other, 'Come on everyone, let's go raid the corn-field!' And there'd be a little one at the back who'd say, 'Um, tell you what, I'll walk and meet you there . . .'

'Earth to Tassie, there's a tour starting now!'

Her dad's shout interrupted her thoughts, and she saw her family in a gaggle of visitors, all elbowing for prime position at the front of the group. Tassie sighed, knowing that mostly what she'd be seeing during the tour would be some fat tourist's back. She watched without surprise as the Twins hustled themselves to the front of the pack, looking as cute as possible, and so deliberately identical that perfect strangers oohed and cooed and ruffled their hair. It was a great performance, and Tassie could only be proud of them. She sighed again, wishing at least one of her school friends had come along for company, but Georgia's eyes had glazed over as soon as she'd heard 'castle', and Benj, like lots of her other mates, refused point blank to get in a car with her dad.

'Oh well,' said Tassie, and with a sudden loud whoop, she threw herself down the grassy slope in a bowling blur of somersaults.

'Cool!' she said at the bottom, as the world spun around her.

Gramma appeared beside her so silently, it made her jump.

'You won't run out of things to do here,' said

Gramma, leaning dangerously on her stick. 'I know Huffington pretty well. I promise to show you something very interesting indeed!'

Chapter 2

Tassie still wasn't convinced that the day was going to be any fun, but at least it was cool in the enormous stone Banqueting Hall. Standing on tiptoe, Tassie could just about see a spotty young man in an 'I Love Huffington' hat. He was pointing at a suit of armour and saying something that sounded an awful lot like 'blah blah blah'. She could also see her dad. She didn't have to be any nearer to know that he had his nose buried in a guidebook, and was giving his own version of the tour to his family. Some pretty fed-up visitors kept saying 'shush' and glaring at him.

Finding zero of interest ahead, Tassie wandered off to the back of the hall, which was covered in old paintings. Most of them were portraits of oddly dressed men with long hair and what looked like white concertinas round their necks. Idly, she cast her eye over the ones at her height – and gave a snort of delight. The glass over the paintings showed her own dim reflection against the background of the person in the picture! So staring back at her was a Tassie in a huge feathered velvet hat with a moustache that looked like a damp caterpillar. She admired herself for a little while, and then moved on to the next one. Now she was a very large, stern-looking matron, sitting atop a gleaming chestnut horse. Tassie thought the poor horse had a bit of a desperate expression, but she was much more interested in how she looked with dark hair piled up on her head, and what her mother's favourite novels might call an 'ample bosom'. Blimey, she thought, I need to get a *lot* taller if *that's* goin' to happen.

'And what do you think of this one?' Gramma spoke from just behind her, making her jump guiltily. But she wasn't looking at Tassie. Her eyes were fixed on a portrait of a young knight, standing beside his white horse. It was a very old picture, and looked rather worn and dirty, as if someone had just found it by accident in a junk room. Tassie could see that the boy's face was sad. With one hand he appeared to be holding up his armoured trousers; the other hand rested on his sword hilt. Underneath the picture was a label that read: *Prince William of Huffington – On the Eve of the Challenge*.

'What challenge?' asked Tassie.

'A joust. His cousin challenged him to a joust. The loser – if he survived – was to be banished to the Crusades, never to return.'

'He doesn't look too happy. Didn't he want to fight?'

'Oh, he really preferred things that were a little less . . . fatal,' Gramma said quietly.

'Well, why didn't he say no then?' asked Tassie reasonably.

'It wasn't allowed in the rules,' said Gramma grimly. 'Once his cousin issued the Challenge, he was, as you might say, stuffed.'

She fumbled up her sleeve a way and produced a grubby lace hanky. For a moment, Tassie thought she glimpsed a chicken-wrap sandwich squirrelled away in the material of the sleeve, but of course she must have been mistaken. Gramma blew her nose like a trumpet soloist, and everyone turned and went, 'Shhhh!'

'He was a sensitive boy, Billy Huffington,' she carried on, regardless. 'He didn't even like hunting much. Oh, he loved horses, but if he came upon an otter or a hare first, he'd shove the thing under his jacket to hide it.'

'But couldn't the dogs smell it?' Tassie was intrigued.

'Oh yes. He needed a lot of new jackets, that boy. He had a nice word for everyone, young Billy. He wrote poetry for his nanny's birthday, and he always gave the castle servants presents on public holidays. His father used to call him a big girl's tunic.'

Tassie choked back a laugh.

'So what happened then?' she asked.

'Well, it was back in the days when Huffington was a kingdom all of its own. Prince Billy's cousin tricked him so he could kill him and inherit the kingdom. And look what happened when he did!' Gramma waved a pudgy hand at the other paintings further down the hall. Tassie took them in, one by one, her trainers squeaking on the stone-flagged floor.

'But they're all so rotten *miserable*,' she cried. And they were. The women's eyes were downcast, the men seemed to hang their heads. Even the dogs that shadowed their masters looked as if they would much rather be somewhere else. 'What on earth happened?'

Gramma strode up to an enormous picture. It was ten feet high, and was framed by golden serpents, writhing together around the canvas. It showed a knight in the blackest armour. A red-eyed dragon snorted on his breastplate, and under his feet lay the bodies of his enemies, their faces contorted in death. The man's eyes were shiny shards of ice, and his lips were drawn back in what he must have supposed was a smile.

Tassie felt the hall grow colder as she noticed that what she thought was the man's helmet under his arm, was actually someone else's head. Underneath

the frame was the legend *Baron Brutus of Badspite –
Gracious in Victory*. She stepped back, shivering, and
Gramma nodded.

'HE happened,' she said.

Chapter 3

Tassie wanted to know more, but Gramma suddenly noticed that they were alone in the hall. The tour had moved on, and the hall was now completely silent.

'Right, Tassie,' said Gramma, hitching her skirt band back up to her armpits. 'Best you get a move on. I think I'll just rest here a minute. Don't you worry about me,' she added as Tassie opened her mouth. 'I know this castle like the back of my hand. Come on, I can show you a short cut out of here if you like.'

She marched up to a tapestry, hanging down next to the big stone fireplace. It showed a rather peculiar hunting scene, with a pack of hounds apparently savaging a young man's jerkin. She used her carved walking stick to pull back the heavy material at one corner and strode confidently under the arch behind it.

There was a resounding *smack*, and Gramma was flat on her back.

Tassie ran to help, trying not to laugh.

'Hmm, they seem to have hung a door since I last came through here.' Gramma didn't sound at all put out, although her nose looked rather bruised. She pulled back the tapestry again. Underneath was an arched wooden door, just about Tassie's height, with cobwebs around the hooped iron handle. Tassie turned it gingerly and looked back at Gramma, who nodded.

'Don't be afraid, Tassie,' she said calmly. She gave just the ghost of a wink and promptly dropped the tapestry.

As Tassie stepped through, she got a really peculiar feeling in the pit of her stomach – as if she was in a lift and the cable had snapped.

'Oh flippin' heck,' said Tassie, blinking in the sunlight. 'Daft old bat has only sent me off outside again.' She tried a quick reversing manoeuvre, but the door had slammed shut behind her, and the latch was completely stuck. 'I'll prob'ly have to buy another ticket to get back in!'

But Tassie knew she could always try smiling sweetly at the man in the ticket office. She wasn't too worried as she sauntered off around the castle walls to find the entrance again. Secretly she was glad to have a little time to herself, without her family causing trouble. The sun was beating down with everything it had, and she kept to the cool shade beneath the towering walls, kicking her trainers through clumps of stinging nettles, and stopping every now and then to look out across the valley. Nothing moved in the midday heat. In fact, it dawned on Tassie gradually, there wasn't anything out there that might do any moving – certainly no cars, or villages full of people. Just an endless horizon of trees and fields and the odd river sparkling like a strip of sweet-wrapper in the grass. It felt weird, thought Tassie suddenly, in the way her school felt weird when everyone had gone and Mum had forgotten to pick her up again. She was just about to carry on round to the gate, when she heard a noise. It sounded like a voice – a nice, well-spoken voice, although she couldn't quite hear what it was saying – and every now and then there'd be an 'OOMPH'. It was the sort of 'OOMPH' that was begging to be investigated, and Tassie was certainly not the girl to disappoint it.

She began to follow the noises, turning on to a little track that veered off downhill towards a nearby copse. She slowed down as she got closer, and the noises got louder. Someone, she could tell, was not having a very good time in those woods, and she was rather anxious not to share it with them. Quietly, she dropped on to all fours and crawled towards a clearing – where the OOMPHing was now more regular than the well-spoken voice – and peered cautiously over a fallen log.

There in front of her was a boy. He had rumpled, straight brown hair and he wore a brown tunic, and what looked suspiciously like tights. He was leaning breathlessly on a long pole, and it was he who was doing the well-spoken talking.

'Well, I say . . . that really is interesting . . . I never

knew that trick, ha ha . . . no, perhaps once is enough . . .!' From across the clearing sprinted a little blur in the shape of a short, chubby man, brandishing a large stick of his own round his head. Tassie watched open mouthed as he ran up to the youngster and wellied him hard across the stomach with it.

'OOMPH!' went the young man and folded like a garden chair.

'Well . . . I . . . um . . . ahem . . . ouch, you know. And everything . . . gosh . . .' He began to rise, still spluttering and coughing from the blow. 'I really . . . um . . . really didn't see THAT one coming . . . ha ha . . . must remember that . . . ha ha . . .'

The short, fat chap was dancing around him, making little growling noises and feinting attacks. He let his victim get almost to his feet, and then, WAP! He delivered a crack round the head that would have stunned a polar bear.

Tassie was very interested to note that the young man's feet actually left the ground before he collapsed sideways. She'd never seen *that* before. But the lad was still burbling on, lying on his back and addressing the sky.

'Mm . . . I can see . . . see how that one could really . . . yes indeed . . . yes most . . . um . . . most painful . . .'

Even growing up with the Twins, Tassie knew the law that said you don't hit a person when they're down (unless there is absolutely no way they'll know who did it). So she couldn't believe her eyes when Shorty started warming up for a sort of golf shot on his helpless victim. Uttering a blood-curdling Ripley yell, she hurled herself over the fallen log and ran full tilt across the clearing. Her head hit Shorty on his backswing, just above the waist, and this time there was a different 'OOMPH', much longer and a good deal louder. He shot backwards under the impact, and somersaulted clean through the bushes and out of sight.

Tassie wasn't even watching. She had grabbed one of the young man's arms, and was hauling him into a sitting position. It was only when she stepped back, panting, that she got a really good look at him.

'Oh!' she said faintly.

'Oh!' wheezed Billy Huffington.

'But you're dead!' said Tassie even more faintly.

'Not quite, but I can see how you might be confused.' Billy put up his hand and felt his head gingerly. 'Oh!' he repeated, looking around for signs of his tormentor. 'You haven't by chance killed my teacher, have you? It sounded like you hit him awfully hard.'

'No, I . . . your *what*?' Tassie was astounded. She quite often didn't see eye to eye with her own teachers, but none had beaten her senseless with a stick. Possibly it was only a matter of time.

Billy didn't notice her confusion.

'It's just that I've got a rather important fight tomorrow, and I'm paying him a lot of money to teach me hand-to-hand combat.'

Tassie gave a short laugh. 'Well, you're obviously not payin' him enough. You were rubbish.'

Billy looked crestfallen. 'Yes. I suppose you're right. You see, I don't actually want to hurt anyone. I thought I'd try a different method. You know, falling over and getting hurt – sort of appealing to his better nature and hoping he'd stop.'

Tassie flopped on the grass next to him and considered this from her own limited experience.

'Well, unless you're fightin' a vicar, I don't think that's goin' to work,' she said finally. 'I think you're goin' to end up gettin' very, very hurt and still losin'.'

'I think I'm going to end up getting very, very *dead* and still losing,' Billy said ruefully. 'My only chance really is to keep my seat.'

'Your seat?'

'On my horse, during the jousting. If we both come off . . .' He waved his hands at his impressive selection of bruises.

'. . . You'll get pasted.' Tassie finished off, absent-mindedly. Her brain was working overtime. There was absolutely no doubt now who this young man was. But what on earth was he doing here? Or, more to the point, what on earth was *she* doing *there*? She suddenly remembered the wink Gramma gave her as she passed through the wooden door. Gramma, she thought grimly, seemed to know an awful lot about the Huffingtons. And Tassie had never met a Medieval Prince before knowing Gramma. There appeared to be a connection . . .

'Joustin'!' she shouted, coming back down to wherever she was on the planet. 'Not against your cousin!'

'Oh you've heard about it then. Zounds, word does travel these days, because you certainly don't look like you're from these parts. How do you get those nice sparkles on your tunic . . .?'

'My name's Tassie. I'm from . . . oh never mind about that now.' Tassie was hot on the trail of the truth, and her spine was tingling with fear. 'Just tell me, who is it you are fightin' tomorrow?'

'My cousin? Oh, Brutus – Baron Brutus of Badspite. He's a bit fearsome, some say, but I think underneath it all he's not a bad old stick – probably homesick I should imagine. I believe it's the custom to kick servants and small puppies in the Badspite highlands, so it's really not surprising he does it here . . .'

But Tassie had stopped listening. '*Not him*!' she breathed.

'*Why* d'you have to fight the Baron?' Tassie finally asked, as she helped Billy to struggle up the path towards the castle. They'd found the teacher among the trees, but when he saw Tassie he said that he was very comfortable in his holly bush thanks, and he might stay there a while longer.

Billy thought for a moment, stopping to catch his breath.

'I'm not *exactly* sure,' he admitted, a puzzled look on his face. 'He turned up here about a month ago, saying he was having a few problems at home and would we mind taking him in until he could get an army together to sort it out. In fact, for several days we kept having Badspitian peasants turn up at the castle gates, waving burning torches and pikestaffs and demanding to see him. Well, he said it was a misunderstanding over tax collecting, so we had the guards ask them to leave.'

'That doesn't sound like any reason to challenge *you* to a joust!' Tassie said.

'No. It was after that. He settled right in and made himself at home. And he is family, so I didn't mind when he had my things moved to Tumbleweed Tower and took over my bedroom. "Brutus," I said. "My home is your home." '

'What did he say?' asked Tassie, suspiciously.

'Um, I think he said, "Exactly Billy-boy." He was jolly grateful.'

'Oh yeah,' Tassie said drily, knowing just what would happen if she ever said to Sam and Lil, 'My bedroom is your bedroom.'

'Well,' continued Billy, holding his bruised ribs as he continued the climb, 'it was about that time that Violetzka came to stay . . .'

Aha! thought Tassie.

'. . . as you've probably heard, she is my Intended, and a sweeter, kinder girl never walked the earth. We are about to be betrothed, and our countries forever united under our rule. When King Pa dies of course.

The uniting thing might be a bit of a problem because Mazovia is almost as far as Prussia but . . . I say! I've written a poem about me and Violetzka and everything. Would you like to hear it?'

'Um . . .' said Tassie. Poetry made her squirm. Billy didn't notice. He put his hand on his heart and addressed the nearest trees:

'Across the sea to marry me,
Came my new Mazovian love.
Amazed was I that she was green!
(The sea, they say, was very rough.)

So fair a maid (though dark on top),
Bewitching-eyed and creamy-eared,
Her laughter makes my heart near stop,
But the way she talks is pretty weird . . .'

'Wow, super,' broke in Tassie. 'I don't suppose,' she continued quickly, 'that you said to your cousin at any point, "My intended is your intended," did you?'

'Well, of course not!' Billy was outraged. Then he turned to look at his surprise visitor. 'You don't think I might have given him that impression do you? Cos that's pretty much what happened. Before I knew it, Violetzka was receiving dozens of red roses in her boudoir each morning, which I'm pretty sure I never sent, and Brutus was taking her for long rides in the country while I was writing my poetry in the orchards. And the *next* thing I know, my cousin has slapped me round the chops with a gauntlet (that's that bruise there – the slightly yellow one) and challenged me to fight for a place at my own wedding!'

Billy had stopped again, and was looking so indignant, Tassie nearly laughed.

'I was REALLY cross!' he finished lamely.

'I bet you were.' Tassie chewed thoughtfully on a long thread of grass. 'It actually doesn't sound to me as if she's worth fightin' for, if she's goin' to run off every time some big hairy brute makes a play for her.'

'Now steady on. None of this is Violetzka's fault. She's just a pure and sweet young thing, too innocent to understand the fix we're all in now.'

She's not the only one, thought Tassie, watching him trip over the long staff he hadn't quite been using to fight with.

'Aren't you a bit young to be gettin' married?' she asked, thinking he didn't look any older than Georgia's big brother.

Billy laughed ruefully.

'I do have such a baby face. No, I am fifteen you know. Pa had fought two wars by the time he was my age. Violetzka says if she's not at least betrothed by the time she's fourteen, she's going off to be a nun, and Mazovia can find itself another princess!'

Tassie opened her mouth but couldn't think of anything to say.

'Actually she's a bit of a handful,' confided Billy, smiling and shaking his head. 'That's the Mazovians for you.'

At that moment they reached the top of the path, beneath the castle wall, and Tassie could see another wooden door. She suddenly wanted very much to see her parents again. She wondered if they'd noticed she was missing, and if her mother had set the whole tour party looking for her. She wasn't going to be popular, that was for sure.

'Well, I really hope everythin' works out for you tomorrow, Billy,' she said, giving him a sort of half wave. She remembered the picture of the unhappy young man in the Banqueting Hall, and felt like a traitor. 'I'm sure you'll beat Brutus.' Ow, that felt even worse. She knew he was going to lose. 'And I expect you'll live happily ever after with your Violetzka.' Wrong, wrong, wrong!

Billy grinned at her happily. 'Thanks old thing. It's all rather exciting isn't it?'

Tassie stifled her guilt, and ran for the wooden arched door. As she did so, she felt a sudden stab of fear. What if she couldn't get back to her own time? For all she knew time travelling was one way only, and she would forever be separated from her family by hundreds of years! Feverishly, she grabbed hold of the iron hoop and twisted it – screwing up her eyes and praying as she did so. For a terrifying moment nothing seemed to happen, and then she had that sensation of her stomach bouncing down to the floor and back up, as the door creaked open wide. A loud 'Gee, that's so cute' was all she needed to know she was back in her own time.

Chapter 4

The mob of tourists was gathered around one end of a huge wooden table that stretched nearly the full length of an enormous, stone-flagged kitchen. Its knotty top was chipped and scarred from the cuts of a thousand cooks' knives, and the Spotty Guide was showing off an amazing array of lethal metal implements.

'Medieval cuisine,' he was squeaking, trying to drown out Tassie's father who had formed a rebel breakaway tour (mostly of visitors who had given up trying to ignore him). 'Medieval cuisine was obviously something of a skill, and there were finely crafted tools for every speciality of the cook's art.'

He groped for a fearsome chopping knife and waved it around to attract attention. The crowd 'oohed' as he nearly scalped Tassie, arriving in the room.

'Tassie!' called Lil. 'Look at me! Look at me! I'm having a barbecue!' She was threading Sam on to an enormous skewer by way of his T-shirt, and trying to drag him towards the roaring fire in a truly cavernous fireplace.

'OK, in a minute,' waved Tassie, looking for her mother.

Mrs Ripley was staring around vaguely, as if she'd lost something. Tassie sidled up to her.

'Don't panic, I'm here. Sorry, Mum.'

Mrs Ripley looked down at her sharply. 'Sorry for what? What have you done?'

'Didn't you miss me . . .?'

'Miss you doing what? Oh please, tell me it's not going to be expensive!' Her mother passed a weary hand over her face.

'No. Nothing . . .' said Tassie slowly. 'You looked worried, Mum.'

'Oh. I was just imagining how long it would take to clean this kitchen floor! We're so lucky we're modern!' She shook her head, tutting.

Tassie squeezed her hand, and then wandered off in search of Gramma.

She was sitting on her own, right at the far end of the dark kitchen, with her feet up on a small stool. From somewhere she had managed to get a tray of tea, and a fire had been lit in the hearth next to her, on which she toasted her tired, mottled feet.

'Oh hello!' she greeted Tassie over her china teacup. 'How was Billy?'

'What . . .? But . . . well, for goodness' sake, why didn't you say somethin'?' hissed Tassie. 'I think you might have warned me!'

'Say something?' Gramma slurped her tea and looked puzzled. 'But didn't I introduce you to Billy in the Banqueting Hall?' She shook her head, trying to remember. 'I know I'm a bit of a Dippy Dodo these days, but I'm sure I told you all about him saving otters and being a big girl's tunic . . .'

'Yes, yes, of course you did. But you didn't actually mention that I was goin' to *meet* him, did you?'

Gramma smiled brightly. 'But I DID say I was

34

going to show you something interesting!'

'But you DIDN'T say somethin' DEAD and interestin'! And why didn't Mum miss me?'

'Can you pass a scone please?'

'There are no scones . . .' Tassie waved at the empty table, and discovered it wasn't.

'With cream – scrummy!' Gramma took a healthy bite and looked at Tassie over her new, white Mexican moustache. 'And have one yourself. No one missed you because you probably left a shadow.'

'How could I leave my shadow? It was with me outside the castle in the sunshine!' Tassie couldn't help having a quick look around, and was relieved to see a long black shape stretched out on the flagstones, cast by the fire. 'Look, it's here.'

'No, it's different. It's a sort of *time* shadow. It's like those cartoons, where people keep running in mid air, even though they've gone over a cliff.'

'Well, how come I even time travelled to start with?' asked Tassie, anxiously, 'and how did I get back, and what would happen if I got stuck . . .'

'Yes all right!' Gramma held up a sticky hand. 'I suppose I do owe you an explanation. I'll give you the simple version because actually it's the only one I understand myself.'

She folded her hands on her lap and stared up at the stone ceiling, as if trying to remember how it went.

'Right,' she said, after a moment, 'let's say that the Past is a balloon . . .'

'A WHAT?' squeaked Tassie, wondering if she had misheard.

'A balloon. And as soon as anything happens it's like a breath going into that balloon, so it's now on the inside . . .'

'Like that second just then?' said Tassie, to be clear.

'Yes. That's now in the Balloon of the Past . . .'

'Or that second when you just said that?'

'Yes, I think you've got the idea,' murmured Gramma. 'Right. The *Present* is always on the outside, so when you get sent back in time, basically it's like pushing your finger into a normal balloon – you can get so far, but the rubbery skin is always trying to push you out again. That's why it's an awful lot easier to get back than it is to go. All you've really got to do is give up being in the Past, and you ping back out again!'

'OK,' said Tassie, after gazing at Gramma open mouthed for a while. 'And so how did I get into the Past to start with?'

'Well, that's because, at some level, you wanted to time travel.'

'Is that all?' said Tassie, horrified. 'So just by havin' a passin' interest in, oh, the Great Fire of London, I could find myself gettin' burned alive . . .!'

'It's not quite *that* simple!' said Gramma, hastily. 'It's MoOD that makes you actually go.'

'I don't think,' said Tassie carefully, 'that I've ever found myself in the "mood" to time travel!'

'No, MoOD. They're . . . well, you really don't want to know. I don't want to know and I work for them! We'll talk about them later when we've more . . . um . . . time. And not on a full stomach. Question is, did you enjoy yourself?'

'No. Well, yes – I mean it was very interestin', but I

felt terrible leavin' Billy there, all brave . . . well, more stupid I should think, but ever so nice . . . and he's not really goin' to die tomorrow is he?' Tassie asked without much hope, because even she knew people didn't win fights by saying 'OOMPH' loudly.

'Course not,' Gramma patted her hand. 'Actually he's going to die in about eight centuries ago – I know I'm mangling tenses but that's Time for you.'

Tassie started to get a bit annoyed. At the opposite end of the kitchen, three castle workers were dragging the Twins away from the fire and trying to put out Sam's T-shirt. And there was that telltale winding-up sound of a Lil tantrum, like the opening notes of an air-raid siren. Her father and the Spotty Guide were fighting for possession of a dangerous-looking meat saw, while her mother had dropped the medieval bowl she'd been examining on the stone floor, and was now trying to hide the broken pieces in her handbag. The other tourists were edging their way to the door. Nobody, it seemed, gave a medieval groat for poor Billy and his long line of utterly miserable relatives.

'Can't you *do* somethin', Gramma?' Tassie asked. 'You seem to know all about it.' She stepped back suddenly as a thought struck her. 'So you must have been there yourself! That's not possible!'

Gramma looked at her, her grey eyebrows shooting up. 'And you swanning around in the thirteenth century *is*, I suppose?' She helped herself to another scone, this time decorating her upper lip with an RAF pilot's handlebar moustache. 'Oh I was there all right,' she said, 'but don't you think I'd have helped if I could? I was a bit . . . inconvenienced you could say. I rather thought *you* might have a go. After all, he's only got another minus a few hundred years and plus several hours to live, and that's not long. Or is it? Well, it shouldn't be.' She looked up at Tassie and winked again. 'You'd better hurry!' Tassie hesitated and Gramma clucked her tongue. 'Come on, or you'll miss all the excitement. I will help if I can. And MoOD is waiting – no, don't ask me about that again now! Just trust me.' She pointed a cream-smeared finger to a door. 'Try that one over there. Something very mystical about doors don't you think? You're never *really* sure what you'll find until you step through them.'

A hundred things crossed Tassie's mind as she turned slowly away. One was the fear of pushing into that Balloon of Time again. She'd never had any call to go messing about in other people's centuries up to now, and it felt just the teeniest bit freaky.

Then there was, 'Just what on earth can *I* do to save a medieval prince?' But finally, and knocking all other thoughts aside like skittles was, 'That bully, Brutus, wants his bottom kickin' from here to Christmas, and I've got Bottom-Kickin' Trainers on!' Tassie lifted her chin and marched for the door to the hall.

Chapter 5

This time the door opened easily – too easily – and Tassie fell through the opening, becoming entangled in the tapestry behind. Flailing out, she heard a sound like a telephone directory ripping in two, and suddenly she was sprawling across the cold stone floor of the Banqueting Hall with the hanging wrapped round her like a toga.

'Flippin' heck!' she mumbled crossly, pushing her hair out of her eyes and trying to sit up.

'WHAT, IN THE NAME OF HUBERT THE HAIR-RAISING HERMIT, IS THAT?' The roar rolled round the rafters of the hall, and made Tassie's ears ring. She stopped wriggling inside the tapestry, and, looking up and around her, saw that the entire room was chock-full of people. Many had their mouths open in horror, and a good few of the men had their hands drawing swords and were running towards her. And at the far end of the hall was a very large and extremely angry-looking king.

'KILL IT!' he roared, pointing at her very rudely.

Tassie had been to enough 'Places of Interest' to know that even historical actors never got this carried away. (One did attempt to burn Lil as a witchlet, at a museum somewhere in the West Country, but Tassie thought he'd had a good point.) Anyway, just staring stupidly with her hair all fussed up from the rug wasn't doing anything to slow down the young men who seemed so eager to make her into a kebab. But those two thoughts, skeetering through her mind in nanoseconds, did give her an idea.

Just as the first knight skidded to a halt beside her and raised his sword, Tassie leapt up into a crouch, threw out both arms to point right at him, and hissed like a cat in a steam bath. What with her wild hair and popping eyes, the effect was magnificent. A little superstition went an awful long way in medieval times, and the knight managed to clear two rows of people in one leap to get away from her. To anyone watching, it looked for all the world as if she had somehow blown him there by magic, and suddenly a lot of bloodthirsty servants of the king were now just scuffling their feet, avoiding her eye and trying to stand behind each other. 'Excuse me, after you Sire . . . I believe you were here first for the kill . . . no indeed my good fellow, I distinctly saw your coat of arms ahead of me . . . ahem . . .'

Tassie was a bit bowled over by her success, but she had seen herself in the mirror in the mornings, and knew just how scary her hair could be. She wasted no time in following up her advantage with a good impression of her mother at her most frightening.

'SSSSS!' she began, with another hiss for good measure, waving her arms around and trying to look much bigger and taller. The knights skittered like nervous sheep and the ones near the back broke loose and legged it. 'Just WHAT do you think you're playin' at, you HORRID . . . MEN you!' The group grinned weakly and there was much clanking as they tried to hide their swords.

Tassie took a step towards them and shouted. 'Toady, batty, foxy, nasty thing with pointy teeth – O!' and stabbed her fingers at them again, flicking her scary hair in a threatening manner. She had her eye on a welcoming-looking doorway just behind the flock.

All this time there had been an increasingly loud rumble coming from the throne end of the Banqueting Hall, and just as the knights finally broke ranks and ran, Tassie saw the king staring at her and getting slowly to his feet. It took an unbelievably long time, as he turned out to be a giant of a man. His black hair hung in massive ringlets like anchor chains, his arms were as thick as beech trees beneath rich velvet sleeves, and his legs were chunks of English oak, knotted and bowed under his silk stockings. The rumbling was coming from deep down in his chest. It rose, even as he rose, and so red and angry was his face that Tassie fancied she could see steam coming from his nose and ears. She blinked. No, it really was steam. His great mouth opened and the roar came surging up, ready to burst into the hall and deafen them all . . .

'And as for you, Mr . . . Mr . . . KING, you!' Tassie held up her hand, as her mother did to show there was no room in this conversation for two. 'Is this the sort of hospitality one expects at Huffington Castle? Hmm? Is this the sort of welcome to give a guest who has travelled so far – or at least for more years than you can imagine – to visit you? Why I've a good mind to turn you all into a bag of earthworms and feed you to the ravens!' ('Yikes!' said one of the courtiers, and tried to exit through an arrow slit.) Tassie shook her head and tutted loudly. 'I'm *really* upset, and *very* disappointed!'

She glared at the king. The king glared at her. And then His Royal Highness burst into tears.

Tassie patted the Royal Head again.

'I've said I'm sorry. How was I to know you're Billy's dad? He doesn't exactly look like you.' She was perching comfortably on the huge carved throne, while the king sat on the step at her feet, his head buried in his hands, and his huge body shaking with sobs. The courtiers and all the knights had suddenly discovered they had very urgent business anywhere away from the Banqueting Hall and the place had emptied like a bathtub. The king gave a deep sigh.

'I was doing so w-well,' he hiccupped. 'I'd called a council of war and everything. I was really getting some respect. You r-ruined it!'

'Yes,' said Tassie, feeling rather awful about the whole thing, 'but come on, you did try to have me killed. And I didn't know you'd been under such a strain recently . . .'

'You have no idea,' the king sounded like a spoiled child. 'No one does. I am Royal, you know. I have Position and Standing, and a hundred and forty-two pages of the Knights' Code to live by. Everyone thinks kinging is having a jolly good time and frightening the peasants. Well, it's not! There are allegiances to make, and enemies to execute, and the parchment work is just endless. And so many decisions! Every day, "What does His Majesty want to wear?", "What does my Lord want to eat?", "Will my Lord require a bath this month?". It doesn't stop!'

'No,' said Tassie slowly, 'I can imagine it's much easier bein' a peasant, with one set of rags, nothin' to eat and no chance of a wash before Christmas. Anyway,' she went on hurriedly, before the king could work out what she meant by this, 'if you think you've got it rough, I was talkin' to your son Billy earlier, and it sounds like he's havin' a far stickier time than you!'

The king heaved an enormous sigh, which moved the sawdust on the floor around a bit.

'Yes, well . . .' he said, uncomfortably, 'I think that might possibly, just maybe, be my fault. Possibly,' he repeated, catching Tassie's stern eye. 'That's why we were having the council of war. We were trying to work out how to stop Billy getting killed at the fight tomorrow.'

'*Why* is it possibly your fault?' Tassie asked, narrowing her eyes suspiciously.

'Well, I sort of asked Brutus to pop over here and toughen the lad up. I mean, I hadn't actually met

Brutus before, but his dad, my brother Bobsy, was always sending over a herald or two to proclaim how he'd conquered another couple of foreign lands, or enslaved a race of ferocious sheep farmers. Apparently he once destroyed a mighty invasion fleet – but if *that* one's true, the invading army was hoping to club Badspitians to death with a decent catch of haddock and a batch of angry octopuses! At any rate, it worried me that my son and heir has done little with his life but pay attention to his schooling, visit the poor – all of it – and fall deeply in love!' The king shook his head sadly. 'A little rampaging never does go amiss in a future monarch, you know. It gives the peasants something to cower at, and make up ghastly folk songs about. I mean, you never hear anyone fol-de-rol-ing about a mighty lord popping in to Old Mother Cribbage to check on her varicose veins, do you? Peasants do like to be afraid of their knights! And the biggest shame . . . almost the biggest shame,' the king corrected himself, seeing Tassie's expression, 'is that Violetzka is the best thing that's happened to our family. She's the last of the Mazovian line and worth millions in beetroot and hunting rights!'

The king's eyes lit up when he mentioned hunting, but Tassie was focused on the important point.

'So you asked Brutus to come over here and give Billy a hard time in the hope that he'd become a nastier person?'

'No, not nastier,' grumbled the king, 'But he is a knight you know. I just think he could do a bit more Questing and a little less Poetry!' Tassie could see he was starting to look a bit sheepish.

'You didn't give Brutus any rules or anythin'? You didn't say at any point, oh, somethin' like . . . make sure you don't kill him?'

'I didn't think it was important. I mean,' said the king hastily, 'I didn't think I needed to spell out that he wasn't supposed to kill my son! It's absolutely unchivalrous, and I shall be having strong words with brother Bobsy when it's all over, believe me!'

'Hmm,' said Tassie, climbing down off the Royal Throne and absent-mindedly playing hopscotch on the chequered stone floor. She bounced down to the far end of the hall, executed a perfect about-turn and smiled at the king.

'Well, I can't see why you don't have strong words with him *before* the fight,' she said. 'Even better, jus' stop the fight?'

'Stop the fight? Stop the fight?' The king jumped to his feet and began to stride up and down, causing little showers of rubble to fall from the ceiling. 'But . . . but . . . but we're KNIGHTS, madam! A knight can no more refuse a challenge than he can do breaststroke in full armour – he could give it a go, but he'd end up looking very wet and silly. And anyway, the law says that if a knight ducks a challenge, everything he has will go to the victor. Brutus will end up being the heir to my throne!'

Tassie stopped on one leg and wobbled a bit while she thought. She'd done a bit of this chivalry-type stuff at school, with King Arthur and the Round Table and all that. If you believed everything you read, truth and purity would triumph over evil, but Tassie knew that low-down cunning was a very handy back-up. She could tell that Billy didn't have a cunning bone in his body, but she was the proud owner of several bagfuls of cunning bones.

'Oh!' said the king, as an afterthought struck him. 'I did do one thing. I put my Sorcerer, Osewald the Obscure, in charge of getting Billy off the hook. It's just possible that magic could solve all our problems! If . . .' he added gloomily, '. . . he could be bothered to do any.'

Sorcerer? thought Tassie. She decided to find this Osewald character right away.

One of the oak doors creaked open, and a wavering voice whispered, 'Sire? Your Majesty?'

'What?' grumped the king.

'I . . . I . . . it's time for your bath, Sire,' came the voice, still frightened, and with no sign of a body being attached to it. It was obvious Tassie's reputation had whipped around the castle quicker than a cold in November.

The king looked despairingly at Tassie. 'You see?

Summer already. What's a king to do when his only son is about to die and he's forced to waste valuable hours washing?' He sighed again and made for the door.

'And can you sieve the water this time?' he shouted at the voice. 'It really isn't funny trying to get lather out of frogspawn.'

It soon became very obvious to Tassie why castles in *her* time roped off all the interesting-looking passageways, and had maps on stands at every corner proclaiming 'YOU ARE HERE' with a big arrow and a red blob. After twenty minutes of searching high and low for Osewald, she was precisely 'NOWHERE', and getting fed up. Every corridor looked the same: damp stone bricks, a couple of blazing torches fugging up the air, and the odd barbaric weapon hanging on the wall, some still with blood on. But no maps. Tassie knew she had a pretty good sense of direction – she'd been lost by her parents on many an expedition in their neighbourhood and always got home all right. Now she was worried, as she rounded each corner, that she might find the old bones of dinner guests of the king who had nipped out to use the privy and never been heard of since.

Without any other reasonable plan, Tassie just kept trundling down passageways, playing 'Ip Dip Sky Blue' at every junction and trusting that sometime soon she'd come upon a door. Or a window. Or even a person! She tried calling out – that had a very pleasing, ghostly echo – and a spot of yodelling, which was fun, and then finally some really loud screaming, like heroines do in the movies when they're FED UP with no one coming to rescue them and can we have a bit of attention here please! Really!

In the end she was rescued by a large pewter jug. It came wanging down the passageway so fast that she was actually nose to nose with it before she saw it and ducked. It was followed by several other ornaments that either bounced off the ceiling and walls with some deafening clanging, or else shattered on impact and continued the flight down the passage in a thousand razor-sharp pieces. They, in turn, were followed, and in some cases overtaken, by a young pageboy holding a bunch of roses.

'Would you be so kind . . .' asked Tassie politely, as he flew towards her, '. . . as to not run past me without stopping, you nasty, rude little boy!' she shouted after him as he vanished into the gloom.

'Oy oy oy . . .' the echo came back. But nothing else did.

Still, *someone* was on the delivery end of all those ornaments, and, dangerous though that *someone* might be, they were still an awful lot better than all the *no ones* of the past half hour. Tassie decided to investigate. Slowly. And ready to duck.

The door was ajar when she got to it, and Tassie listened very carefully before pushing it open and stepping into the room. It wasn't quite what she'd expected. In the first case, the room was enormous, and sunlight poured through two large windows that looked out across the courtyard to rolling hills beyond. After the gloom of the passages, Tassie's eyes immediately began to water – not very useful when you know there's a murderous fast-bowler somewhere in the room with you. And whoever was in here was really overdoing it with the perfume.

'I . . . don't . . . vant . . . zem!' It was a girl's voice, and she wasn't having a good day. She hissed out the words as if her teeth had been welded together.

'Fine!' said Tassie, blinking furiously to see where the voice had come from. 'Because I haven't got them!'

There was a pause, and the sound of someone flouncing impatiently off a feather bed. 'You say so? You lie!' That was pure sulk now.

'I do say so!' said Tassie firmly, because she didn't have *anything* except the clothes she stood up in. 'And,' she continued because she didn't like being called a liar by anyone, 'if I *did* have them, I certainly wouldn't give them to *you*. So there.'

Another pause. Tassie's eyes were beginning to clear now, but she gave them a few extra rubs because she couldn't quite believe what they were showing her. The entire room seemed to be full, from floor to ceiling, with roses of every size, shape and colour. They stood on the floor in pots, they leant on chairs in bouquets, they wound up the pillars of an enormous four-poster bed, and they rambled across the ceiling and round the windows. Some were even trying to escape up the chimney of a king-sized fireplace. Tassie couldn't see the owner of the voice for flowers. Then, all of a sudden, there emerged a girl, not much older than Tassie herself. She had beautiful dark hair, plaited and curled on her head, flashing dark blue eyes, and a thunderous frown of the sort that curdles milk.

'Zow art not Stewart!' she said, accusingly.

'Stewart?' asked Tassie, trying to waft the overwhelming scent of roses out of her nose. 'I'm sorry, can we open a window? Oh,' she added as she noticed there was no glass in the windows anyway.

'Stewart ze Steward. Zow art not Stewart ze Steward!'

'The boy that nearly flattened me in the passage? Is that really what he's called? Poor bloke!' Tassie sniggered. 'What did you do to him?'

A small smile sneaked across the girl's face, but she stamped on it immediately with a heavy scowl.

'He brought to me more roses from zat odorous oaf,

57

Brutus. So I pressed zem with some vigour down ze back of 'is tights and zen zrew ze pot after 'im.'

'Aha!' said Tassie thoughtfully. 'Then you must be Violetzka. But aren't you goin' to marry Brutus?'

There were some peculiar noises that Tassie took to be medieval curses.

'Over my dead body,' finished Violetzka, punting a ceramic bowl angrily out of the window and hitting a passing pigeon.

Tassie smiled. 'But hopefully not Billy's,' she said.

'Ah Billeee!' sighed the girl, throwing herself on to the bed, and staring dreamily out of the window. ''E is such an 'andsome dish, no? 'Ave you seen him? Does 'e speak of me?'

'Yes,' said Tassie carefully, 'you got a mention.'

'Vot did 'e say? Am I still 'is beloved?'

'Well, he did seem a bit put out about you gettin' all these flowers from Brutus. And then there were the long rides in the woods. What else? Oh yes, he was partic'ly upset to discover he had to fight a duel to the death for a place at his own wedding.'

But Violetzka was already on her feet, wringing her hands in the manner of a distressed maiden – although it did sound more like she was cracking her knuckles for a fight.

'A duel? No! A duel of ze vords perhaps?' she cried hopefully.

Tassie shook her head, trying to pick at a rose spray that had snagged her T-shirt.

'Afraid not,' she said. 'As far as I could tell it was the "knock you off your horse, big scary sword and spiky ball on a chain" type of duel Billy was practisin' for.'

Violetzka stared at her in horror. 'No! 'Ow was 'e?'

'Pretty damaged by the end of it.' Tassie jumped on to the down-soft feather bed. 'Ouch!' she said. 'Is there a pea under this mattress?'

'No, I took it out zis morning. Stupid fairy tales!'

'Mm, must be a thorn then. Anyway,' Tassie continued, bouncing up and down and doing an experimental somersault, 'how did all this happen? I really don't want Billy to die, and I don't think you do either – although I was very cross with you

59

when I first heard what you'd done.'

'Me?' squawked Violetzka indignantly. 'I do nussing! It is all zat brutal brute, Brutus! 'E ask me von evening, "Violetzka, how does a knight woo his lady-love?" And I tell him, "vell, you can never send her too many flowers," and suddenly kazamnitch! I am SUFFOCATED viz roses! Ven I voke zis morning, I 'ad roses growing up my leg! I HATE roses! And viz every new bunch of roses I get ze same stupid message. "Flowers for my flower, kiz kiz kiz!" I tell you ze man is driving me completely strudel-cakes! My poor sick papa sends me 'ere for ze betrothal and ze love and ze good alliance with Huffington zat vill bring my people into ze thirteenth century, and vot happens?' She threw her arms up and tutted. 'My Billee is slappered round ze chops viz ze Challenge! And I myself?' She drew herself up majestically. 'I am just ze prawn in all zis!'

Tassie thought about this as she bounced. 'You mean "pawn", don't you?'

'I mean messed about like ze old baggage!'

'Well, why didn't you jus' tell Billy that you're not

interested in Brutus?' Tassie asked, managing to slip a half-twist into her next backflip.

The frown on Violetzka's face blossomed almost purple with rage.

'Tell 'im? I 'aven't even SEEN 'im for a fortnight! I can't find my way out of ze stupid guest ving! Five times I have set off down zat corridor. Ze last time I vos lost for two days before I ended up back 'ere! Look!' She turned around and pulled the pins from her hair. A dark rope fell down her back. 'Just anozzer six months and I vill be able to escape out of ze window down my own hair!'

'Brutus must have told Billy that you wouldn't see him until after the Challenge. Surely Billy wouldn't fall for that?'

The two of them looked at each other.

'OK then,' said Tassie. 'We need to find a way to escape.' A thought struck her. 'Does Brutus ever come to this guest wing?'

Violetzka gave a short laugh.

''E used to come and visit, but 'e discovered very

quickly zat ze roses made 'im viz ze sneezey-wheezey and ze itchy-scritchy, and now 'e cannot come 'ere! It is ze only reason I don't zrow ze 'ole stupid lot out of ze stupid window!'

'Really? That's very interestin'. Very interestin' indeed . . . well, at least he won't be interruptin' us then.' Tassie took a deep breath and executed a backflip dismount from the bed, with barely a wobble on landing. She raised her arms to take the applause. 'Come on then, Violetzka,' she said. 'Billy needs our help!'

'And so to the Great Courtyard,' read Tassie's father from his guidebook, as he led the sweating group of tourists out into the sunshine. He peered over his glasses at some stragglers. 'Excuse me . . . you . . . no, not you . . . the fat one next to you. No madam, fatter than you . . . yes! You, sir. Would you mind not talking while I'm reading? We don't do that in England. Thank you so much.'

The Spotty Guide had put up a grand fight, but the end had finally come when Mr Ripley had accused him of going the wrong way and then led the group down an unexplored tunnel that just happened to come out in the Banqueting Hall. Talk about jammy. (Although some of the Americans had got quite shirty when they realised the tunnel was actually the chimney.)

The tourists milled around the courtyard, savouring the fresh air. Lil had persuaded Sam to put his head and hands in the stocks, and was now sitting on the top bar to keep it shut, inviting everyone to kick his backside as they passed. Recognising Mr Ripley's son, quite a few obliged, even at the price of a pound. But the tour wasn't over yet.

'This beautiful piece of stonework here is a fifteenth-century coffin – alas, Victorian thieves and body snatchers made off with the contents, and the carved gold lid . . .' said Mr Ripley, completely ignoring what the guidebook said.

'Gee!', 'Zut alors!' and 'Blimey!' said the tourists, clicking their cameras.

'It's a water trough!' muttered the Spotty Guide, mopping his face in a shady corner. 'Hey everyone, it's a water trough . . .'

'And if we all turn to the Tower of Torture on my right, you can clearly see . . .'

'My daughter!' screamed Tassie's mother, pointing upwards. 'That's my daughter!'

The crowd went 'Ooh', and even the people trying to escape over the ramparts came running back to have a look.

Tassie was having a trying time. She and Violetzka had spent hours picking the thorns off some pretty vicious rambling roses, and plaiting the stems together to make a sturdy rope. When Tassie had peeked out of the window, all that lay below was a large, stone courtyard, with a couple of bored-looking horses tied up near the coffin-shaped thing in the corner, and one of those jousting practice machines that bashed you over the head if you forgot to duck. Having got a third of the way down the make-do rope, she now discovered that the courtyard contained about thirty gawping tourists, an ice-cream stand (closed) and a large plastic map with 'YOU ARE HERE', an arrow and a red blob sketched on it. She was descending, feet first, into her own century. The Balloon of Time was pushing her out! That was cheating – she'd gone out through the window, not a door!

'Whoahohoh!' wobbled Tassie on the rope.

'Tassie!' screamed her mother. 'What on *earth* do you think you're doing? That T-shirt is just out of the wash!'

Tassie looked up desperately, hoping she might wriggle back up the rope into the tower room, but the rope just petered out into nothing a few feet above her, and Violetzka's anxious cursing had faded to silence. Nothing for it but to carry on down and bluff it out. If she was a little slow in her descent, it wasn't for a fear of heights; rather it was the fear of what would happen when she hit the ground and her mum got hold of her and shook her till her teeth fell out. She knew she needed a devious and very convincing plan . . .

Four feet from the ground she shouted, 'Look! There's a badger!' and let go with one hand to point dramatically over the crowd's shoulders. While the crowd, amazingly, turned round and jostled for a good view, Tassie jumped the final distance to the ground. Without even pausing to say 'Oof!', she scrambled away through the legs of the tourists and towards a small, almost hidden gate in the castle walls that she'd spotted on the way down.

'I am pretty sure that's actually just a pigeon,' said a disappointed American.

Tassie wriggled harder. She knew that people in ye olden days were quite a bit smaller than her generation, but the gate arch had narrowed almost to the size of a rabbit hole! She managed to get her head and one arm through into the daylight beyond, but then she was stuck fast. Nose in the mud, she waited, panicking, for her mother to start yanking her back by the ankles. There was far too much to be done in the thirteenth century to be wasting time here. She hoped Violetzka had made it safely out of the tower in her own time. So wrapped up was Tassie in the Middle Ages that when she heard, 'Oh! Hello there!' in a ridiculously cheery voice, she knew it had to be Billy. This gave her the sudden worrying thought that her bottom half was at least eight hundred years adrift from the bit with the brains.

'Mmff,' said Tassie muddily – looking like a swimmer caught doing the front crawl when the tide went out.

There was a pause.

'Super evening!' Billy tried again. He was obviously in the mood for a chat.

'Mmmmfff. Mmfffmm!'

Another pause.

'Why are you trying to crawl through our cat-flap?' asked Billy. 'I say, would you like me to give you a hand or anything? You look like you might be stuck!' There was a clanking noise and a great deal of grunting, then Tassie felt a metal hand grab her wrist and give it a couple of gentle tugs. She was just about to give up and try going backwards, when Billy gave an absolutely almighty heave. She shot out of the hole so fast that she knocked Billy flying, and ended up sitting on his chest, rubbing her sore arm and checking her legs had made it into the Middle Ages.

'Wow, you look smart!' Tassie exclaimed, admiring her reflection in Billy's shiny armoured breastplate.

Billy pushed up the visor that had fallen down over his face.

'I'm going to have my portrait painted,' he said proudly. 'Actually, I've only hired this suit for the joust. I haven't worn my old set since I was twelve, and it took two village blacksmiths and a jug of goose-grease just to get one spaulder on! And it all rode up in a really horrible way . . .' he added with feeling. 'Anyway, King Pa fixed up an artist to do the Great Work – said he thought it would be rather jolly to have something to remember me by.'

That rather spoilt the mood, thought Tassie.

'Oh! Look at that cloud formation!' said Billy, pointing at the sky. 'Don't you think it looks like two squirrels kissing?'

Just then, a man in a smock with an easel under his arm came ambling round the corner of the castle. He saw Billy and bowed low.

'Greetings, your Royal Knightness. I am ready to begin the portrait!' He leant forward and whispered confidentially, 'I believe my lord might look more noble in the standing position.'

In the end they had to roll Billy on to his front so he could crawl to the nearest tree for a bit of leverage. Tassie joined in to help, while the painter squinted at the sun and measured his thumb against the horizon, and bent Billy's limbs into a pleasingly manly pose.

'So there you are.' Tassie couldn't help putting in her farthing's worth about the joust. 'You've jus' been thumped out of the saddle by several tons of Brutus and his horse. He has time to dismount, sharpen his axe, have afternoon tea and prob'ly learn the violin, and you're STILL lyin' on your back like a wounded tin of salmon, just waitin' for him to put you out of your misery!'

'Big smile Your Princeness!' called the painter from behind his canvas.

Billy managed a sort of lop-sided grin.

'Come on old thing. It won't be as bad as that!' he jollied, out of the side of his mouth.

'Yeah – if you don't turn up. It's your only sportin' chance.'

'And let that scoundrel get away scot free with Violetzka and my kingdom and everything?'

'Violetzka doesn't want you to get killed fightin' for her, you know. She told me!'

'Of course she doesn't. That's exactly why she's worth fighting for. I can't let Brutus just waltz off with her. Over my dead body!'

'So everyone says.'

'Sorry old girl, but the pride of the Huffingtons is at stake here. King Pa would have twelve different breeds of kittens if I skipped the fixture! He heard a boy at my Knight Class call me "Huff the Puff" once. That was four years ago, and on a quiet evening you can still hear that boy screaming!'

Tassie gave up. Secretly she really admired Billy for sticking to his guns. (That's an idea! No . . . if anyone at Huffington in her time actually *had* a gun, they'd have used it on her dad by now.) She was better off trying to stop Brutus killing him, than stop Billy committing suicide in such a terribly English way. She needed to find Osewald the Sorcerer.

'Can you hear somethin'?' she asked suddenly, cocking an ear in the direction of the woods.

Billy looked nervous. 'No. What something?'

'I don't know. A sort of crashin'-through-the-undergrowth somethin'. And a sort of howlin' . . .'

'Oh no . . .'

All of a sudden the treeline at the bottom of the hill erupted in a foaming of scruffy coats, waving tails and whiffling black noses. The dogs surged up the slope like a spring tide, and as they caught sight of Billy there was a great baying and howling and scrambling over each other.

Billy turned to run. He'd actually managed to get one foot in the air when the tidal wave broke over him and he went down, screaming, under the pack.

It was over in seconds. A small brown nose peeked out briefly from the neck of Billy's breastplate, and then the otter pinged like a little treacle-coloured arrow, out between the frantic back legs of the pack and towards the open fields. It was followed, seconds later, by the baying mongrels, and then by two men in leggings with hunting horns. They waved their fists briefly at Billy, and disappeared, puffing after their motley hounds.

Billy lay still.

'It's actually not half so painful with armour on,' he said reflectively. 'Hope the little chap gets away.' There was another pause. 'I don't think I'll try saving polecats with this on. Bit snug.'

'Well,' said Tassie, when they'd got him upright, dusted and looking noble again. 'I'd better get goin'. By the way, do you know where Osewald the Obscure is at the moment?'

'Oh, he had a message that his mother needed him urgently up north. Poor chap, he couldn't pack fast enough! He said it was such a shame, just as King Pa had asked him to give me a helping hand and everything.'

'Yes, what a coincidence,' said Tassie under her breath. She sighed. She'd been quite looking forward to trying some magic.

'Oh well,' she said to Billy, 'I'll see you later, Baked Potata. I need to find Violetzka again!'

Tassie walked off past the painter and sneaked a look at his work.

'Where's the white horse?' she asked, leaving the painter scratching his head and muttering, 'A white horse! Now *that's* a good idea!'

assie needed to find Violetzka quickly, but she wasn't sure how. She paused in the courtyard to get her bearings. It was dusk now. In the stillness of the evening she heard a laugh, and then someone striking up with a stringed instrument, and some rather tuneless voices.

'Well, someone in there must know how to find the guest wing!' thought Tassie, heading for a thick oak door. Through it she could hear a great deal of shouting, and singing, and the clattering of pewter mugs and slamming of plates on tables. They must be making merry before Sir Brutus plunged Huffington into misery tomorrow, mused Tassie. She knew medieval parties were usually riotous because table manners hadn't been invented then. With some hesitation, she pushed the door open a crack.

The noise stopped so sharply, she thought she'd gone deaf. It wasn't a very nice kind of silence either – it was sort of like the one just before her science teacher threw her homework at her. Or that really tense, frightening silence between Dad coming home and Dad discovering the Coca-Cola sloshing round in the keyboard of his PC. Still, 'faint heart never buttered no parsnips', or whatever her mum's saying was, and so Tassie took a deep breath and kicked the door open wide like a sheriff raiding a dodgy Wild West saloon bar. As she did so, she felt the centuries lurch, and the now-familiar sensation of having her stomach sucked out through her belly button for a nanosecond. The old oak of the door morphed into modern frosted glass and a surprised Tassie was just able to read 'Ye Castle Cafe' etched in squiggly script across the middle before the door slammed back on its hinges and shattered into a thousand pieces . . .

'Oops,' said Tassie, which didn't really cover the situation. She looked up warily at the room full of fellow tourists, expecting the barrage of shouting and fuss that usually followed such disasters. Thirty pairs of eyes in the queue at the hot counter turned to stare at her . . . and then thirty pairs of eyes looked back sourly at their trays. Tassie felt slightly aggrieved. It had been a top class smash-up but it was only getting the stony, frigid silence of people who were seriously wound up about something – or someone – else.

'Tassie! Where the heck have you been?' her father shouted happily from the front of the queue, rubbing his hands. 'Come on down here. I've been saving a place for your mother and the Twins too. They had to go to the loos because Sam tried to eat the chewing gum he found in his hair and he's just thrown up all over Lil . . . and that Spotty Guide.'

There was the sound of knives and forks being slammed down in disgust by those already tucking into the hot quiche pie. The Spotty Guide was standing just behind Mr Ripley and had obviously been well sponged down. He glared murderously at Tassie's father from beneath his dripping fringe.

'Can you just . . . hurry . . . up . . . sir!' he ground out. 'Other people are waiting for their lunch.'

Mr Ripley frowned.

'You've just heard me say I'm waiting for my wife. And what's your problem? You don't see these people complaining!' He flung out an arm to indicate the long line of customers behind him, foaming with silent fury as their soup congealed in their bowls. His flourishing hand hit a tray and put the contents neatly across two rows of diners. Mr Ripley was too busy eyeballing the Spotty Guide.

Tassie realised she must act fast. Quickly, she helped herself to a ready-wrapped cheese-and-pickle sandwich.

'Er . . . if you don't mind, Dad,' she said, edging away, 'I'll jus' go and sit down way over there somewhere with Gramma. Thanks, bye.'

'Phew,' she said, blowing her fringe up in the air as she clambered into the seat opposite Gramma. The old lady was already up to her ears in a large chicken drumstick, and Tassie watched, startled, as the meat disappeared as if up an industrial vacuum cleaner.

'Erm,' she said, blinking at the demolished drumstick. 'I've got an idea to help Billy!'

Gramma waved one hand around frantically and made short, angry grunting noises.

'Well, I thought you'd be pleased,' said Tassie, tired and annoyed. She crossed her arms in a sulk. Gramma went purple and started thumping her chest.

'Bone . . . stuck!' she croaked, between choking fits. 'Help . . . yeech . . . agony . . .'

'And I haven't seen you in the Past yet,' carried on Tassie, kicking her legs and glaring at the ceiling. It did seem like she was doing all the dirty work while Gramma just enjoyed herself.

'Dying . . . bone . . . can't . . . breathe . . .' Gramma groped around for her walking stick and, flailing wildly, managed to thwack herself hard across the back. A sharp piece of bone shot from her mouth, missed Tassie by millimetres, and embedded itself in one of the nearby quiche lunches. The knives and forks went down again with a clatter. Gramma reached calmly for another chicken leg.

'I've go' somefing for you,' she said, swallowing another mouthful. 'Might come in handy. I think you should be running along now . . .' she continued as Tassie frowned. 'No time to waste and all that. Lives to save, derrings to do.' Gramma passed over a grease-stained piece of paper, and turned her attention to a biggish slice of strawberry cheesecake. Tassie was just about to unfold it when voices over by the hot counter started to rise rebelliously.

'It's just a shame that the rest of the world doesn't understand how to queue!' came Mr Ripley's peevish voice from within the scrum. 'Excuse me, that's MY beef casserole thank you very much. Yes, I know it wasn't on my tray but I'd already baggsied it. What? Baggsy? Well, it means the casserole is mine even though you actually got hold of it first . . . yes, it might not sound fair to a foreigner, but I'll just take that if you don't mind . . .'

There was the crash of thirty trays hitting the floor

at the same time, and a mighty roar echoed round the stone hall. Before Tassie could decide whether to run to help her father, or to run as fast as possible in the opposite direction, her mother and the Twins appeared in what was left of the doorway. All three wore knights' helmets bought from the Olde Gifte Shoppe on the way back from the loos, and the Twins flourished wooden swords with evil intent.

'And what,' boomed Mrs Ripley, pushing up her visor and making the rioters spin to face this fresh threat, 'do you think you're doing to my husband?'

'You get off our dad or you'll be sorry!' shouted the Twins in unison, and Sam jabbed his sword into the nearest tourist's leg to emphasise the point.

'Aargh!' went the man.

'Banzai!' screamed Mrs Ripley, waving her cardy like a battle flag.

'Get them!' howled the tourist mob, any remaining self-control in shreds.

'Yeeeehooo!' whooped the Twins as they fell upon the enemy with huge enjoyment.

Tassie thought four Ripleys were more than enough to take on the crowd.

'Bye, Gramma,' she said, but Gramma was already on number ten of her after-lunch forty winks.

As the armies came together, mid-café, Tassie ran straight through the middle of them, bouncing off bellies and bumbags, until she hit the kitchen door like an American footballer on a touchdown. She felt the years slip, sickeningly, as she somersaulted to a messy halt on the other side.

'Invasion!' shrieked a fat woman in a cloth cap, and threw a pail of water over her.

Chapter 9

The kitchens in Billy Huffington's day weren't nearly so spick and span as when the tourists had nosed around them. A number of worried-looking young girls with lank hair stuffed into caps ran hither and thither with their arms full of vegetables and mixing bowls. The air was heavy with heat and grease and steam, and a small boy turning a pig on a spit in front of the great fire was getting a better crackling on him than on the roast.

Sitting on the floor, Tassie's mouth goldfished with the shock of the cold water, and she glared at the large woman. The woman put her shovel-sized hands on her hips and glared back. There was a stand-off for a couple of moments, until a pot on the fire started to rock dangerously and screech steam. Then the woman threw back her head and yelled, showing teeth as stumpy and rotten as a derelict pier.

'Aggie! Aggie! Yer gormless gin-wutted chislet! Pitcher tha pot! Aggie!'

When there was no response, she reached back with an arm like a sumo wrestler's thigh and lifted the pot off the flames and on to a cooling shelf. The pot handle was sizzling hot and all aglow, but the woman didn't seem to notice, despite the sudden stink of frying flesh.

Tassie gulped.

'Now me lutty chiglitter, wis ya poochin un ma cretch?' the woman demanded. 'Eh? Histy gutta tongchamper? Hodi slick dondown me lutty tigbadger? Hm? Hm?'

Tassie stared at her in a sort of terrified surprise. The last thing she wanted to do was upset this monstrous mountain of a woman any further so she cast around for a soothing reply.

'That's a rotten speech problem you've got there,' she tried.

The woman turned a purplish colour and, seizing a

huge meat cleaver from the table, swung it high in the air, sending different zones of her body into a frenzied wobble. Trained by the Twins to expect the unexpected – or even the worst – Tassie was up and over the table a full half a nanosecond before the cleaver hit the floor.

'Sorry! Sorry!' shouted Tassie, scattering bowls, boards and kitchen wenches as she slid off the far side of the table. 'I expect you must be Scottish then!'

Her attacker screeched with fury and snatched another cleaver from the rack on the wall. It embedded itself, twanging, in the pillar next to Tassie's head.

'Well, where *does* she come from?' she asked one of the kitchen maids rather crossly as they both jostled for a safe position under the table.

The girl looked at her wearily and tapped the side of her head.

'The mad'ouse,' she said in a slow, country burr. 'She's the 'ead Cook.'

'Really?' asked Tassie, thinking she wouldn't want anyone quite so murderous in charge of her daily food. 'She must be very good!'

'She ain't that good at the cookin' side, but she be brilliant at killin' anyone trying to get rid o' her.'

'Oh. Right. Tell you what,' whispered Tassie, looking around for an escape, 'how about you go out over that way, and I'll cover you.'

The girl shook her head firmly. 'In my right ear, lady! I got a ma and fifteen sisters to support!'

Tassie gritted her teeth. Sometimes it got jolly boring being the only kid on the block with a bit of gumption.

'OK,' she said tiredly. 'I'll run out and draw her fire and you can run away back to your ma.'

'Don' be daaft!' said the girl. 'Who do you think we be hidin' from?'

'Cooee ickling trubbers!' The voice was wheedling now, trying to lure them out. Tassie found herself revoltingly close to the lower half of a thick set of legs, stuffed into a pair of wooden clogs.

'By the way,' Tassie asked, as she screwed up all her courage and concentrated on not being sick, 'which way is the guest wing?'

The girl pointed at the far door, up a set of worn stone steps.

'Thanks,' said Tassie, and, taking a deep breath, she sank her teeth into one of the mad lady's calves. Then she struck out, hell for leather, towards the door as the shrieks echoed round and round the stone-flagged kitchen.

'That be where Master Brutus lives,' said the girl in her slow way, 'so I reckons the guest wing is ower *thatter* way.' She pointed in the opposite direction. 'Oh. She garn!'

Chapter 10

It didn't take long for Tassie to work out that she was going in the wrong direction. For one thing, there were no young stewards or vases hurtling along the corridors, and for another, her T-shirt had become terribly tight around the neck. Her feet, though still walking, had lost contact with the stone floor, and there was an extremely unpleasant smell coming from just beside her. She turned, as far as the T-shirt would allow, and came face to face with the most massive armpit she had ever seen in her life. It had a collection of muscles that seemed the size of a biggish mountain range, but with a lot more hair, and a truly diabolical aroma.

'Aha!' said a deep voice from above her. 'A fresh one! And they'd told me they'd run out!'

'Ngffnagh,' answered Tassie, kicking and wriggling.

'Nffghwygh mndwffght.' The pressure round her neck disappeared all of a sudden, and her feet hit the floor again, followed immediately by her bottom. She turned slowly, and looked up, then up further, trying to find the top of the giant figure that towered above her. He was clothed almost entirely in leather straps and tights, with so many muscles bulging that he looked like a pile of rubble sacks tied together. His jet-black hair was long, and braided into a pigtail at the back, and his beard had been somehow filed into several points. Even though he no longer had someone's decapitated head under his arm, Tassie instantly recognised his steely eyes and cruel mouth as he bent down for a better view.

'Zounds, what a weird-looking insect,' said Baron Brutus of Badspite, which Tassie thought was pretty rich coming from him. He had breath like rotting fish, and it made the hairs in her nose curl up. 'What form of life can it be?' And he prodded Tassie curiously in the shoulder. Terrified or not, Tassie wasn't having any of this. She jumped to her feet.

'Sir Brutus, I presume,' she said in her most polite, detention-avoiding tone. She tried a curtsey, remembered she couldn't do one, switched it in mid-dip for a bow and had to clutch a tapestry for support.

Brutus stepped back in alarm and drew his sword.

'I called for a new servant and they send me this . . . this tadpole instead! I should kill them all for their insolence!'

'Oh, but I am your new steward,' said Tassie hastily. 'Or is it a serf? Could be a squire. It's all too many S's, isn't it? I jus' got a bit lost, you know how it is with castles. Although *you* seem to have made yourself at home!'

Shut up shut up shut up shut up, her brain shouted at her mouth.

'That is true,' said Brutus, after eyeing her suspiciously for a minute. He sheathed his sword. 'And I suppose that a half-grown frog is better than nothing when there's a joust in the offing. Take my armour and follow me!' And he threw a size XXXL breastplate and helmet for her to catch – which she did, but only because the floor caught her.

In the Great Courtyard, lots of worried-looking servants were running around lighting torches, until it seemed as if the whole square was on fire. When they saw Brutus, they cowered and whimpered; when they saw what looked like a giant tortoise following him, they dropped everything and fled. The tortoise stopped and Tassie crawled out from under the armour. 'Are we nearly there yet?' she gasped, rolling on to her back and squinting in the light. The great shadow of Brutus appeared across her face, together with a metal boot that appeared painfully in her ribs.

'All right! Chill, Bill!' Tassie jumped to her feet and made an effort to spruce up and look squire-ish.

Brutus didn't seem to notice. He'd started a show all of his own.

'Tonight,' he shouted, pacing up and down and waving his fists at empty windows and battlements, 'tonight we hone my jousting skill to a razor edge!' Tassie looked around to see who the 'we' might be. Whoever it was, they were late on parade.

'And tomorrow, as you shall see,' hissed Brutus, villainously, 'Huffington may rejoice in a new heir, and a NEW... CHAMPION!' The chilling words rang around the silent courtyard, over the bare ramparts, and echoed across the still, dark peasant fields.

Tassie looked around again. Two horses, one white, one black, stood facing each other at either end of the courtyard. She looked at them; they looked at her. She looked at Brutus. Brutus looked at her.

'Absolutely, totally, and without a shadow of a doubt, no,' she said firmly. 'No way, no chance, no how. You can get lost. No.'

'Tadpole,' grinned Brutus, tickling her chin with the tip of his sword, 'you'll find your armour and lance beside the horse. Best you hurry, lest I start before you are ready.' He turned and began to walk towards the black stallion.

'But you see ... much as I'd love to and all that ... I can't actually ride!' explained Tassie, not moving.

'You won't be on the horse long enough for it to matter.' Brutus kept walking.

'But I'm much younger than I look. Way too young to die . . . by, oh, quite a few years!'

'The smaller the target, the better the practice,' said Brutus, turning around with a sneer.

'The trouble with bad guys,' grumbled Tassie as she dragged her heels over towards the white horse, 'is that they're always so flippin' BAD! And what are you lookin' at?' she snapped at the horse, which stared at her curiously as she picked up the pile of small-sized armour.

'I'm not sure. It hasn't got a label,' said a voice.

'What?'

'It's not what, it's pardon. And I said, it hasn't got a label,' repeated the voice. 'I believe that's a joke from round about your time, although I could be a few decades off. The old noggin isn't what it used to be . . . will be. Whatever.'

Tassie stared at the horse. 'Gramma?' she whispered, not believing her eyes and ears. 'Gramma? No way!'

'Way,' confirmed the horse comfortably. 'What? You think you can only time travel in human form?'

'Yes . . . no. I mean, I *never* really thought about it. Until now that is . . .' Tassie gaped and tried to collect herself. 'Well, I can see why you couldn't . . . can't . . . help poor Billy on your own!'

'No. It's a bit restricting. I've tried talking to him, but no one here expects conversation from a horse so they block it out. And it's not like I can even teach him how to ride properly. I mean, he does take me out, but only so we can walk side by side through the trees while he tries out his poetry on me! I now know a lot more about rhymes for "Violetzka" than he ever will about a rising trot.' Gramma shook her mane in irritation. 'Anyway, I don't want to worry you, but it looks like Sir Brutus is ready to start the practice. Get your armour on . . . no, not like that, that's upside down . . . no, now it's inside out – how did you manage *that*?'

'This is all a bit pointless,' said Tassie, puffing her way into the breastplate, 'cos as soon as his back's turned, I'm runnin' away as fast as my little legs can carry me!'

Gramma shook her head.

'I'm afraid that won't work. Firstly, he's just locked all the doors and gates to the courtyard. Secondly, he'll kill you. Thirdly, I'm afraid when he's finished killing you, he'll come back and kill you some more.'

This was not music to Tassie's ears.

'Never mind,' said Gramma, 'listen to me. I've done lots of these practices with the old brute, and it always ends up with the squire in bits on a stretcher because they will insist on panicking. You *musn't* panic! Just let him knock you off my back a couple of times and we can all go home in one piece.'

Don't panic, thought Tassie sturdily. There was the pounding of approaching hooves on the gravel behind her, and a fiery snorting filled her ears. Her knees turned to lemon jelly as the hooves screeched to an impressive halt.

'It's time for the first joust, Tadpole,' roared Brutus. 'I'm sure you'd feel more comfortable if you were sitting upon your horse!' And he pushed his lance in through one of the armholes in her breastplate and out through the other, hoisting her into the air like a shirt on a clothesline.

Tassie regarded him balefully as she swung to and fro.

'If you wouldn't mind puttin' me down, MR Brutus,' she said coldly. 'I'm sure you'll find that danglin' people in their armour is not what you knights might call "shivery"!'

'Chivalrous,' corrected Gramma out of the side of her mouth.

'I *do* beg your pardon,' sneered Brutus, tipping the lance so she slid off on to Gramma's saddle. 'But I so like to see my fish before I fillet 'em!' He kicked his horse and galloped off to the far end of the courtyard, spinning the beast to face Tassie. Tassie, in the meantime, was trying again and again to pick up her lance from where it leant against a wall. It was about four times her height, and very heavy.

'Remember what I said,' breathed Gramma as they lined up beside the jousting rail.

'No, what?' Tassie couldn't take her eyes off the

creature opposite, for the black of the horse and the black of Sir Brutus's armour merged into one snorting, pawing, smoke-breathing monster, and even the light of the flaming torches sank without a trace into the darkness of its coat. 'I s'pose I'd be right in aimin' the pointy end of this thing at Mackerel Breath over there?'

'Don't . . . panic!' repeated Gramma soothingly. 'Just concentrate . . . focus.'

Then, 'Oh my God!'

'What? What?' cried Tassie, nearly passing out with nerves.

'I think I left the iron on!'

'What?' screamed Tassie.

'I knew something was niggling at me! It'll burn right through that pretty blouse Help the Aged gave me last Christmas. Bother!'

'Gramma,' said Tassie tightly, and between teeth clenched like a bear trap. 'As you have about eight hundred years to sort that disaster out, can we just look after the little matter of me still bein' in one piece half an hour from now? Hmm? I mean, it's not as if you're plannin' to wear that blouse this evening, is it?'

'It's a jolly nice blouse,' grumbled Gramma to herself moodily. 'I've only just managed to get the chocolate sauce out of it from the Gentle Folks Tea Dance and Karate Weekend.'

Tassie gritted her teeth, took a firm grip of the lance with both hands, and a rather less secure grip of Gramma with both knees.

'Are you ready, Tadpole?' shouted Brutus, raising his lance with a flourish.

'Come on then, if you think you're hard enough!' Tassie yelled back bravely, and with a whoop she jammed her heels hard into her horse's flanks. 'Hit it, Gramma!' she cried, and Gramma did.

There was a sort of roaring noise in Tassie's ears, and a frantic pounding that could have been her heart, or the hooves of the steeds as they hurtled towards each other. Tassie was hanging on for dear life. The black monster seemed to get bigger and bigger, faster and faster, until Tassie just closed her eyes and felt the world spin upside down . . .!

'Get,' snarled Brutus, 'off my horse!'

Tassie looked up at him, a little confused. And then she looked behind her, and found his horse's face turned to glare at her. Then she looked down. She was sitting on the black beast's neck, and clinging on to Brutus's armoured legs.

'How did . . .?' she began slowly.

'You shimmied up my lance,' said Brutus. 'I don't know how you did it . . .' he bent his head down until they were nose to visor, '. . . but it is STRICTLY AGAINST THE RULES! CLEAR?'

'Gosh, it's a long way down!' said Tassie, peering over the side. 'Do you think you could help me . . .? Ouch,' she said, as Brutus tipped her on to the ground, hard.

'I really don't think this is very sportin',' Tassie complained while Brutus roped her ankles together under Gramma's belly. The Badspite Knight grunted as he pulled the knots tight.

'Urchin,' he said, 'you are mistaking me for someone who gives a fig about "sporting". Practice I want, and practice I shall have.'

'But if you hit me now . . .' Tassie tried to move her legs and failed. She gulped.

'I am not inhuman,' sniffed Brutus. 'I will make sure all parts of your body are collected and buried in the same place.' He stalked off back to his own horse, clanking in an irritated way.

'Well, you've done it now!' said Gramma, miffed. 'What am I going to tell your mother? She'll never take me out again.'

Tassie's mind boggled for a minute as she imagined the conversation over her bloody corpse: 'And how did this happen? In the thirteenth century, you say? Yes, I am quite cross. Oh well, I dare say it couldn't be helped. Can you just pick up that severed arm for me . . . thank you.' She shook her head to clear it. Must be the concussion. That ground was really hard . . .

Suddenly, a smile spread across Tassie's face. She'd had an Idea, and it was a Jolly Good One – way better than being smeared across the courtyard like strawberry jam!

'Gramma! Listen!' she commanded excitedly. She leant forwards and started whispering in her horse's ear.

'When you've QUITE finished with the long goodbyes,' shouted Brutus impatiently, 'I hate to hurry you, but I have an urgent meeting this evening to sell off some local peasants.'

'Don't be ridiculous. You can't sell peasants!' said Tassie, in disgust.

'Actually, at this moment you are correct,' agreed Brutus amiably, 'but after my victory tomorrow, I think you'll find I can.' He gave an evil, echoing chuckle. 'And I do so want to be ready!'

'But . . . but . . . the king wouldn't let you do that to his subjects!' cried Tassie.

Brutus laughed, the nasty, deep rolling laugh beloved of baddies everywhere.

'Ah, the poor dear king!' he said, shaking his head sadly. 'God rest his soul.'

'What do you mean?' demanded Tassie, narrowing her eyes at him. 'What's happened to him?'

'Oh, nothing yet,' said Brutus airily. 'But I hear he's in a life-threatening condition.'

'Which is?'

'Standing between me and a very large amount of power and wealth. Now that is *never* healthy!'

Tassie couldn't believe her ears! The man was actually threatening the ruler in his own castle! Suddenly she realised how slim poor Billy's chances were of coming through the Challenge alive. And it made her very angry.

'Mr Baron Brutus of Badspite,' she started in a low and dangerous voice. 'I didn't like you before I met you, and I'm likin' you less and less every minute. In fact, if I like you any lesser, you're goin' to disappear altogether, and that would be just fine by everyone!'

She swung the heavy lance up and into position, and then drew herself up to her full height, which didn't take long at all.

'But before that happens, and because you're SUCH a wrong-un, I'm goin' to give you the pastin' you deserve!' she cried, and dug her heels into Gramma, who squealed in surprise and shot forwards like a streak of white lightning.

'*Banzai*!' screamed Tassie, as was the Ripley way, her hair streaming out beneath her helmet.

'Death to the half-frog!' roared Brutus, digging in his spurs and charging to meet her.

The two bore down on each other like express trains. But this time, Tassie's eyes were wide open, and shining with the sort of expression that always made her mother get the first-aid kit ready. She saw the drumming black hooves stampeding towards her. She saw Brutus's evil face, half-hidden by his visor and the pointy beard, and she noticed how his black lance was levelled straight at her, ready to blast her into a week next Thursday . . .

'Now!' she yelled, and Gramma stopped dead in her tracks. Only the rope around Tassie's ankles stopped her from whizzing over the horse's head, and possibly over the castle ramparts. She pretended to fumble with the lance, and forced the blunt end deep into the ground until it was hard against a rock. Brutus bore down on her . . . closer . . . closer. When his massive figure blotted out the whole courtyard, she ducked sharply under his lance and angled her own point at the snarling dragon on the Baron's metalled chest. When Brutus hit her lance it wasn't a rather skinny eleven-year old who held it – it was several million tons of Planet Earth.

There was a CRUNCH, like a barrel of snails being hit by a truck.

'Blimey!' said Tassie, hugely impressed, as Brutus sailed up and over in a wide arc, apparently attached to the tip of her lance. 'Awesome!' she breathed, as it slammed him head first into the ground. 'And serves you right!' she chirped happily, as she untied her ankles. She dismounted and strolled over to the crumpled heap to administer a good kick where the armour didn't quite meet.

'I will never . . . ever . . . fall for that again,' said Brutus, muffled inside the dented helmet, 'and if you tell anyone, I shall hunt you down and kill you slowly. You are no longer my squire.'

'Humph!' said Tassie. 'Funny old thing, MR Brutus, but you don't scare me half as much as you did a few minutes ago. I take it the practice is over?' And she walked off, dusting her hands in satisfaction of a job well done.

Five seconds later she came back.

'Um, can I have the key to get out of here please?' she asked meekly.

Chapter 11

I can't go in there. I'm a horse,' said Gramma, as Tassie tried to lead her into the castle.

'Well, I'm not leavin' you out there with Mr Crumply. He's not goin' to be too happy when he gets his breath back. Anyway, I don't think a horse would make the top ten of weird things people have seen in this castle. They probably won't even notice you.'

'All right,' said Gramma, clopping loudly on the flagstones. 'Where are the kitchens? I'm a tad peckish.'

'Definitely not,' said Tassie firmly. 'Not unless you want to be horse-burgers. I'm not flavour of the month with the Head Cook. And she didn't taste too good either,' she added, gagging at the memory.

As a matter of fact, Tassie was feeling sick anyway. Her insides were jangling like a washing line in a hurricane. She knew it must be the Balloon of Time trying to push her back to her own century. She clenched her brain and pushed back until her head swam and the feeling faded away. Triumph over the Balloon! For now . . .

'Well, how about your plan then?' said Gramma. 'Don't I remember that you were going to tell me about a plan before, later?'

'What?' said Tassie, confused. 'I do have a plan, but I need to find Violetzka. Have you any idea where we are?'

'No,' said Gramma. 'But you have.'

'Me? No, I'm as lost as anything.'

Gramma tutted. 'Didn't I give you a piece of paper yet? I'm sure I did. Will.'

Tassie slapped her hands to her jeans pocket.

'I forgot all about it!' she cried. 'It must have been the excitement of everyone tryin' to kill me!'

'It's a map of the castle,' said Gramma. 'I pinched it off the Spotty Guide while he was trying to strangle your father in the kitchens. It should give us *some* idea where on earth we are . . . what are you eating?'

'Cheesh 'n' pickle,' mumbled Tassie round a mouthful. 'I jush found it in my pocket with the map. It's a bit squished . . . oh go on then.' She sighed, handing over the package to Gramma. 'Don't eat the clingfilm . . .! Ah well, I'm sure it won't hurt you.'

When the last scrap of the packet had disappeared, the two of them studied the map by the light of a wall candle. Tassie held it up, while Gramma breathed heavily over her shoulder. After a few minutes Tassie turned it up the other way.

'I think we're round about there,' said Tassie eventually, jabbing a finger vaguely at the bottom of the paper. 'Maybe. What do you think?'

'I don't think anything. Horses can't read maps,' said Gramma. Then, when Tassie rolled her eyes, 'I'm sorry, my dear. But if I could do everything myself I wouldn't have had to ask you along!'

'I don't remember you askin'.' grumbled Tassie. 'Threw me to the ravenin' wolves is more like it.'

Gramma looked hurt.

'I thought you were up for a bit of fun,' she said, and set off down the passageway with a sort of exaggerated limp to show she had been wounded.

Tassie felt ashamed, even though she knew Gramma was putting it on. Truth to tell, she *was* enjoying herself. OK, the jousting was pretty scary, but she hadn't actually been that much more frightened than when the Twins had buried her up to her nose in the sand at Yarmouth, and gone off for an ice cream while the tide came in. And it beat every other Ripley day out by a landslide. She scurried after Gramma.

'Let's forget it,' she said, which would have passed for a grovelling apology in her family. 'Would it be all right if you gave me a lift for a while? I'm so tired my legs are goin' to drop off.'

'OK, but get rid of that breastplate,' said Gramma, her good humour instantly restored. 'It's like carrying a fridge-freezer around.'

And the two of them continued on their uncertain journey into the bowels of Huffington Castle, with Gramma slipping and sliding on the damp stones, while Tassie lit the way with the candle she'd fixed on to her little helmet. They plodded on without speaking for a while until Tassie broached the subject that had been bothering her.

'Don't you think it's about time you told me what this MoOD thing is?' she asked casually. 'If that's what's behind all these weird goings on. I expect it's goin' to explain quite a bit about why you're a horse and stuff.'

'Oh yes, I suppose you should know who the boss is,' said Gramma grimly. 'MoOD stands for "Ministry of Other Dimensions". Basically it's the Ministry's job to keep an eye on History and make sure it behaves itself. I work for them – sort of a field agent so to speak. There are agents all over the place in History. It's our job to try to keep things ticking along on an even keel and step in to stop some of the stupider things that might happen, like world destruction or school dinners.'

'But . . .' started Tassie.

'. . . I didn't say we always succeeded,' said Gramma testily, 'but I do think world destruction was the best one to get right. Anyway, you wouldn't believe how much mess History can get itself into. And we're very short of staff.'

'Well, why were you sent here as a horse then?' asked Tassie, trying to stop candle wax dripping on her nose. 'I mean, you said yourself there's not much you can do with a saddle on your back.'

'Oh, you think that I came here to sort out Billy's problems, don't you? Why do people always think the world revolves around humans? I actually came on a serious horse matter, and it was only when I got here I found out about the mess Brutus and Billy were in. I thought I'd need a bit of help.'

'Really?' asked Tassie, rather proud. 'And what did MoOD say?'

'They said, "Yes, if you're careful, but don't let any of those other Ripley lunatics loose in Time," ' Gramma snorted.

'Cool!' said Tassie, even prouder. They trotted along for a minute while she thought about all this, then she asked curiously, 'What are they like, the

MoOD people? Do you ever see them?'

'Oh yes,' said Gramma in a low voice that echoed strangely in the passageway. 'Normally when I've messed something up.' She gave a huge shiver. 'And what makes you think they're people?'

'Aren't they?' Tassie was taken aback.

'Sometimes,' said Gramma darkly.

Clopping along in a dark, damp corridor, several centuries from home, Tassie's mind was racing so much that she missed the time-slither in her stomach. Suddenly they had arrived back in the future Banqueting Hall.

'There's another of the little thugs!' shouted a burly policeman, spreading out his arms and advancing on Tassie. 'Attack an old lady would you, you little monster.'

Tassie blinked at him and looked down. Gramma the horse had vanished from underneath her, and in her place was the original, twenty-first-century Gramma, all white blouse and generous skirts, spread-eagled face down on the floor and looking for all the world like a bushwhacked pensioner. Tassie leapt off her back in a good impression of a scalded cat.

'Um,' she said. 'This *reeeally* isn't how it looks.'

'I'll just bet,' grinned the policeman nastily, picking up a chair and jabbing it at her like a lion tamer. The hall was filled with strobing blue lights and the cacophony of what sounded like a thousand police sirens. Through the open castle entrance, Tassie could see groups of cowering tourists with their hands on their heads, queuing up to be searched, while the Law, in full riot gear, brandished sticks and shields. And there was still a battle royal going on in various parts of the hall.

Tassie backed away.

'Tell him, Gramma!' she hissed.

'Wheeeeeeze!' said Gramma helpfully, without moving.

'The poor old bird, I reckon you've done for her!' said the policman in horror, and strengthened his grip on the chair. Tassie thought quickly, remembering that attack was almost always the best form of defence.

She straightened up and put her hands purposefully on her hips, wondering only fleetingly if she still had a candle stuck on her helmet.

'Well, DUH!' she said, giving the word its full portion of scathing contempt. 'She certainly will be done for if you don't let me carry on givin' her heart massage!'

'What?' said the copper.

'My gran's got a . . . a dodgy ticker,' said Tassie, a little hazy on medical details. 'When she gets overexcited her heart stops, and I have to . . . er . . . massage it. You know. Give it a jump start.'

The policeman peered at her more closely.

'Hang on, you look just like those two awful young . . .'

'Look! I think she's turnin' blue!' shouted Tassie, leaping back to Gramma's side and giving her a few hearty thumps between the shoulder blades. Gramma groaned and sat up.

'Thank you, angel,' she said, glaring daggers at Tassie. 'You saved my life again. She's such a brave little thing,' she continued to the copper, all innocent.

The policeman dropped his chair to the ground and then sat on to it, mopping his brow.

'Well then. I'm sorry,' he said. 'It's been a dreadful afternoon. It's put me right off having kids I can tell you. Or visiting castles!'

Looking around, Tassie could quite see why. The noise was deafening. Most of the suits of armour displayed in the hall were now strewn in bits across the floor. The painting of Billy had skewed to an interesting angle, so that he looked like he was falling over in slow motion. Here and there, bewildered policemen were trying to calm screaming tourists by sitting on them hard, while the big American had managed to claw his way up a tapestry to a safe ledge, and was bellowing into his mobile phone.

'I wanna speak to the American ambassador . . . no, right now . . . some Brit has just declared war on us and I've got a constable wrapped around my leg!' He kicked vigorously, and the pyramid of Boys in Blue trying to reach him gave a nasty wobble and collapsed like a sack of spuds.

'See what I mean?' said Tassie's policeman dismally.

'Mm,' said Tassie. 'Er . . . what exactly is *he* doing?' She pointed into a corner, where the Spotty Guide had taken up a battleaxe and was attacking a thick oak door with it. Everyone was busy pretending not to notice him.

'Oh yes. There's a family that's barricaded itself in the turret, and I think he wants them to come out,' said the policeman.

'Really? That wouldn't be those lovely Ripleys, would it?' asked Tassie innocently.

'Yeah. Do you know them?'

'Not really,' said Tassie slowly, 'but they were ever so nice to us when we joined the tour. That horrid guide took against them from the start. The last time I saw him he was throwin' a beef casserole at the dad!' she finished truthfully.

'Really? Can't say as I blame him,' said the policeman with feeling. 'The two Ripley brats locked three of our men in the ice-cream display cabinet before giving us all the slip. We had to send the dogs in!'

'You set the dogs on the children?' Tassie was shocked.

'*After* the children – most of the dogs are now being looked at by a vet. Two of the coppers have frostbite, and one's having his stomach pumped after over-choc-icing himself.'

'Tsk,' said Tassie sympathetically.

'Choc-ices?' said Gramma, with interest.

'I expect the children were frightened,' Tassie got in quickly. 'You really frightened me when we came in. And me just doin' my first aid and everything.' She trembled her lower lip and looked at her feet. Gramma gave a pathetic cough and thumped her chest. It was a masterly performance.

'Yes, well, if only all kids were like you,' said the policeman, patting Tassie kindly on the shoulder. 'And if only people knew how to behave like they did in your time,' he said to Gramma.

'Which time?' asked Gramma.

'Hello . . . who's this now?' The policeman stood up as a young man sauntered through the castle entrance. Despite the fact it was still about twenty-eight degrees outside, his grey mackintosh was buttoned up to the neck, and he wore a hat pulled low over his eyes.

'Can I help you, sir?'

'Sure. Can we go somewhere more kinda private?' asked the man in a quiet American accent, jerking his head meaningfully at Tassie and Gramma.

'Oh, you must be CIA!' said Tassie with excitement. 'They always turn up at war zones. Cool! Can I borrow your gun?'

The man sighed.

'Right. Now the young lady has blown my cover, I believe you're holding a United States citizen here somewhere? I've come to bail him out.'

The policeman looked over the stranger's shoulder to where the American visitor was busily stamping on any Long Arms of the Law that got a grip on his ledge.

'I rather think he's holding us,' the copper said sourly, 'and if you want to remove him, you'll get three rousing cheers from the Huffington constabulary. Do please help yourself.'

'Roger that,' said the CIA man. He went to walk past Tassie and stopped.

'Don't look now, kid, but you've got a candle on your head.'

Chapter 12

Left alone again in the midst of all the mayhem, Tassie and Gramma held a council of war.

'Well, I don't see why we have to rescue them!' said Tassie mutinously. 'They're jus' embarrassin' me as usual. We've got enough on our plate with poor Billy. If we don't do somethin' soon, Huffington is goin' to be Misery Central for the next few hundred years.'

'They are your family, dear,' said Gramma, 'and family always comes first.'

'But I'm *always* gettin' them out of trouble,' said Tassie. 'Have you got any family, Gramma?' she asked curiously.

'More than you can shake a stick at,' she said grimly. 'And I've shaken plenty. However, none of them are here at the moment, thank God, so let's talk about your family. At least let's go and see if they're OK.'

'Fine. Jus' one eensy weensy problem with that,' said Tassie, nodding. 'Captain Join-the-Dots over there with the nasty big axe. He's nearly through the door too.'

Indeed the Spotty Guide was now standing amid a pile of wood, which he continued to attack ferociously with the axe, muttering, 'It's a water trough, you hear me? A water trough!' through sobbing breaths.

'Well, you just pop over and talk to him, there's a love. I'll be with you in a minute. I think the elastic's just gone in my drawers.'

'What? But I'm just a kid! What can I . . .'

But Gramma had disappeared under her skirts for a rummage. Tassie stared at the heaving pile of laundry for a moment, and then threw up her hands.

'Right. I'll do it. Again. You'll be sorry when I'm dead!' Grumbling, she dragged her heels over towards the Spotty Guide, carefully avoiding two tourists trying to give each other Chinese burns.

''Ang on a mo!' The tourists fell back from each other, panting, and one waved her over as he caught his breath. 'Do us a favour will you, luv? 'Old me mobile while I give this idiot a good drubbing.' He only just managed to pass it over before his opponent sent him flying with a rugby tackle. Tassie looked at the phone. She punched some numbers in. She walked over to the Spotty Guide while it rang at the other end.

'Yes, what?' shouted an angry voice in her ear. Tassie tapped the Spotty Guide on the back.

'S'cuse me,' she said politely, as he whipped round, raising the axe. She offered him the phone. 'It's for you.'

'Oh . . . um . . . thanks.' The Spotty Guide put down the axe and leant on it. 'Hello? Hello . . .? I'm sorry, who is this?' His eyes unfocused, and he began pacing aimlessly about.

Tassie looked back to signal Gramma that the way was clear, and was almost bowled over by a clothing parcel moving at high speed towards the broken door. It stopped on the first step up to the turret, and Gramma's beaming face emerged from the skirts.

'Well, don't just stand there,' she said. 'Chop chop chip shop. Scooteroo.'

Halfway up the steep winding staircase, they could hear both sides of the phone conversation.

'Oh it's you, is it?' snarled the Spotty Guide from below. 'Why don't you come down and fight like a man?'

'Ha!' snorted Mr Ripley from above. 'Find me a man to fight and I will.' (Rousing cheers from the background.)

'Just you wait till I get through this door!' threatened the Spotty Guide, oblivious to the fact he had already destroyed most of it.

'Ya ya blah blah. You talk big for an Acne Factory,' scoffed Mr Ripley, and then to one side, 'look, will you lot just shut up a minute? I can't hear myself insult him. Sam! Sam! Put that down before it . . . ouch . . . well, there, see? Anyone got a plaster?'

'Come down here right now and I'll let your family go,' shouted the Spotty Guide.

'When we come down, you'd better be a long, long way away, hiding under a bed and saying your prayers, mister.' (More cheers.)

'I'm going to give you two minutes. If you're not out by then, you're going to get a proper spanking. I'm starting to count now. One . . . two . . . three . . .'

'Hang on a minute! That's too fast! You're supposed to say "rickety basket" after every number. That's a proper second.'

'Oh. OK. One (rickety basket), two (rickety basket), three (rickety basket) . . . you still there? . . . four (rickety basket) . . .'

'That should keep him busy,' said Mr Ripley, sticking him on 'Hold' and putting the phone in his pocket. 'Right, what the heck do we do now?'

'Hi, Dad,' said Tassie, appearing on the top step.

'Tassie!' cried the family.

'Billy,' gasped Tassie. A small door had opened at the far end of the room, and Billy was emerging, head down and rolling up a parchment with 'The Last Will and Testament of Goode Prince William' in fancy script at the top. At the sound of his name he shot a couple of feet in the air and collapsed gasping against a sturdy wooden table.

'By all the Imps of Ippingham!' he managed. 'I say old thing! Do you have to scare a bod like that?'

'What on earth are you doin' here?' asked Tassie.

'That revolting guide chappy chased us up here,' said Tassie's mum. 'Why have you got a candle on your head, dear?'

'Not you, Mum, him!'

'I . . . um . . . that is . . .' Billy gave a quick glance behind him, where the open door revealed a garderobe, one of the castle loos.

'Him who?' Tassie's mum and dad looked around, puzzled, and Sam and Lil tapped their heads, crossed their eyes and sniggered.

'No, I mean what are you doin' *here*?' said Tassie to Billy, eyeing the parchment that he was trying to hide behind his back.

'I told you dear, there was a bit of a kerfuffle between your father and . . . er . . . everyone else really . . .'

'Well, I needed somewhere to collect my thoughts before bed, and King Pa says he has all his best ideas in the privy,' said Billy, looking shamefaced. He seemed oblivious to everyone but Tassie – and Gramma, who had finally arrived, wheezing, in the room. He patted Gramma on the head in a friendly way. 'I didn't know there was a queue outside. Jolly sorry and all that.'

'Did you see the spotty bloke with an axe on your way up?' asked Tassie's father, peering anxiously over Tassie's shoulder.

Tassie's head was spinning.

'Er . . . can everyone jus' wait here a second while we go and . . . er . . . sort things.' Ignoring the odd looks she was getting from them all, she grabbed hold of Gramma (who had only just caught her breath), bundling her back out of the room and halfway down the stairs.

'What's happenin'?' Tassie hissed. 'Can't they see each other?'

Gramma thought a bit.

'It's because they are still in their own centuries, so they see what they expect to see. It's just us – we've gone and overlapped ourselves. Sometimes that happens when you're going back and fro too quickly. Time takes a while to catch up.'

Something clicked in Tassie's brain. 'And is that why Billy patted you on the head? He only sees you as a horse?'

'I do so hope that's the reason. Actually, I'm getting confused myself. I very nearly bit him!'

'Well, what are we goin' to do?' asked Tassie, pinching her lip. From down below she could hear the sound of the Spotty Guide approaching the two-minute deadline.

'One hundred (rickety basket), one hundred and one (rickety basket) . . .'

'How about if we all go back to the thirteenth century to hide from the guide? Would that work?'

Gramma looked embarrassed. 'Mmm,' she said without enthusiasm. 'Although that is *possible*, I'm afraid it's against the law.'

'What do you mean by "against the law"? This is an emergency!' Tassie hissed.

'Yes, but think about it. MoOD are *really* strict

about time travel. Otherwise you could just imagine the mess History would be in. For instance, what would happen if your father just popped in at the Battle of Waterloo?'

Tassie was horrified by the picture that conjured up.

'OK, I get that. But they let *me* travel. Wouldn't MoOD let them – jus' this once?'

'But you're licensed. I went to MoOD and pleaded your case, and they gave you a special licence to see how you got on.'

'Wow. Well, we can do that for Mum and Dad and the Twins, can't we?'

'No, we can't. First of all, I've only just been to see them about you, and one meeting a century is one too many. Secondly, if you remember, MoOD said that there was absolutely no way the rest of your family would be let loose in time. No way, no how.'

'OK then,' said Tassie stoutly. 'I s'pose there's nothing for it. We'll jus' have to lock them in the privy and hope for the best.'

'One hundred and twenty (rickety basket)!' finished

off the Spotty Guide downstairs. 'Hello? Hello? Are you there, Mr Ripley? Right, that's it!' he said furiously, slamming the phone into a corner. 'Coming, ready or not!' And then there was the terrifying sound of a large battleaxe being dragged up stone steps.

Tassie gulped. 'I think we've jus' run out of time,' she said, starting for the turret room at a run. 'Come on, Gramma!'

Upstairs, Mr Ripley had made everyone remove most of their clothes, down to their underwear, and was trying to knot it together to form a rope for escaping out of the window. He tied one end around the iron hoop door latch, and leant back hard to test it. For a moment all was well, then Lil's purple lycra leggings parted at the seams with a sound like a swarm of bees blowing raspberries. Tassie's dad hurtled backwards (passing right through Billy, who gave a puzzled shiver) across the room and through the privy door. When his family rushed in to help, they found him firmly wedged on the stone long-drop toilet, with his wife's skirt wrapped round his head.

'George!' cried Mrs Ripley. The Twins fell on the floor and screeched with laughter.

Billy, left on his own (or so he thought), decided to slope away. He felt that he'd rather let Tassie down by creeping off to make his Will, when he really should be grinding a razor edge on his sword and reminding himself which end to hold. He headed upstairs, just as Tassie came steaming in the opposite direction.

'Snerfle!' exclaimed Billy, bowled sideways.

'Oops, sorry! I . . . er . . . I need to use the "little room",' said Tassie, seeing that her whole family was already crowded in there trying to free Mr Ripley from both the skirt and the toilet in which he was stuck fast. 'Look, Billy, I think you should get off to bed now. My mum always says that troubles don't look half so bad in the morning.'

'Right ho,' said Billy, trying to sound cheerful. 'She sounds like a very wise woman. I'll be off then. Night night.'

'Goodnight, sleep tight,' Tassie cried, haring past him, followed closely by Gramma, who was an interesting shade of puce. He watched them dash into the toilet together, and the door slam shut.

'Gadzooks,' thought Billy, staring for a moment in surprise. 'I think she might be spoiling that horse.'

He carried on down the stairs, and shivered again as the Spotty Guide coming the other way passed right through him.

'I think you'll be fine if you jus' stay in here for a while,' said Tassie to her dad. 'Lie low and keep quiet. That oak door is pretty solid.'

'Humph. It's not like I have a lot of choice, is it? Not until we can get my bottom out of this seat anyway,' said her father grumpily. 'If it all ends badly, promise me this won't get into the newspapers.'

He'd managed to disentangle himself from his wife's skirt, but now wore it around his neck like a colourful Arab scarf. The rest of the family made an interesting picture too, crammed into the tiny privy in vests and pants.

'Gramma and me are goin' out now,' Tassie said briskly. 'I want you to lock the door behind me! The guide is on his way up, and I think he's managed to get a sword from somewhere as well as the axe.'

That should hold 'em, she thought to herself.

'Can't we come with you, Tassie?' asked Lil, bouncing up and down eagerly. 'We'd be a LOT of help!'

'You know we could be LOTS of help!' added Sam, pogoing in time with his twin. 'Come on. You know we could!'

It always amazed Tassie how they could sniff out mischief and adventure in the offing. In fact, she would have quite liked to take them, if it had been allowed.

'No,' she said firmly, 'you'd only cause trouble.'

The Twins were shocked breathless by this thoroughly fair accusation.

'Would not! You just wait. Bet you need us soon!' retorted Sam. They tried to rush Tassie at the door, and she had to fend them off with both hands.

'Right, we're goin' now,' she said, slamming the door on their yelps.

'Where are you going . . .? Tassie! . . . I said, where are you going? Don't you dare leave until I . . .' said Tassie's mum. '. . . OK, well, come back soon!' she ordered through the closed door. 'I was hoping she could dig up a cup of tea from somewhere. It must be well past four o'clock.'

Outside the door, Tassie and Gramma waited nervously while the sound of metal on stone came closer. They both blew out a huge sigh of relief when a distinctly medieval knight hauled himself into view at the top of the stairs. He stood there for a moment, red in the face and clutching his armoured sides.

'I . . . so . . . wish . . . they put a privy in . . . closer to the stables,' he spluttered. 'It's such a bind when you've spent the day out Questing and . . . oh I say! You came up by horse – what a *super* idea!'

Gramma, once more her four-legged shape, nudged Tassie with her nose and waved it at the window.

'It's getting late,' she whispered. 'I hope the Plan

you mentioned is of the "very simple and not too time-consuming" sort.'

'Well, if we're too late,' said Tassie, scrambling on to her back, 'can't we just go a bit further back in time and be early?'

'La la la, not listening!' trolled Gramma, rolling her eyes and clattering her hooves on the floor. 'What did I say to you about using common sense with time travel? Just leave it alone!'

'Excuse me,' said the knight, recovered. 'Can I squeeze by? I'm back out Questing in two minutes.'

'Oh.' Tassie remembered her family as they passed him. 'Er. I wouldn't go in there. It's rather badly blocked. If you know what I mean.'

The knight glared bitterly at Gramma's departing rump. 'Oh yes, I know exactly what you mean! Thanks a lot!' And he started the long hike back downstairs.

Tassie had the map out again as they trotted down the stairs, but when they passed through the Banqueting Hall they were distracted by loud voices at the far end.

'Well, it be the thin end o' the wedge, yer Madgisty,' said one gruff peasant voice, so rural Tassie could almost *hear* turnips. 'The mucky end o' the stick, the mould in that there cheese, the maggot in the venison . . .'

'Yes, thank you, Bilge, I am still eating if you don't mind,' said the king, pushing a quail around his plate moodily and wondering how the Unwashed had managed to get in past the guards.

Twelve pairs of hungry eyes followed the quail's progress.

'Sorry, yer Huffingtonness. I forgot. We finished our

dinner three days ago. Anyway, Sire, 'tis not that we mind a bit o' disease and starvation under a king as generous and . . . and . . .'

'Beneficent,' hissed his wife. 'I 'eard it in a proclamation.'

'. . . generous and beneficent as yer good self,' carried on Bilge the peasant, trying not to drool over the quail. ''Tis just that when the Baron of Badspite's men came round puttin' "For Sale" notices on these 'ere children just now, me missis 'ere were a bit upset.'

The missis gave a mighty sniff and dabbed her eye.

'But, Zounds man, there's ten children! And look, not all of them have notices.' The king sounded a bit huffy. He was annoyed with his nephew because selling people's offspring was definitely against the Knights' Code, but he felt he had to back him up against the peasant riff-raff.

''E's snagged every child without the Plague,' said Bilge firmly, 'and with poultices at near a penny a throw, *they're* not like to last long.'

'Plague?' inquired the king faintly.

'Well, somefin' with revoltin' sores anyway. Coupla me boys keelin' over like swoonin' maidens, they are. Prince Billy's doin' wonders with a vermin paste though. Germlin – show master yer sores.'

'Yikes!' said the king, as a small, grubby boy from somewhere behind his chair, exhibited a big, purple swelling under his rag shirt.

'Course, our Billy . . . I mean, Prince William . . . has been an absolute Golden Turnip – always givin' out old sheets for bandages, and enough milk to keep their strength up . . .'

'Has he indeed?' mused the king, who'd slept on straw for a week and eaten his morning oats dry. 'I must remember to congratulate him.'

'. . . so 'tis a bit upsettin''-like for the Poor that not only do it look as if Prince William'll be bowin' out o' public life . . . well, bowin' out of *any* life I s'pose . . . but that there new man'll be makin' off with our lovable little tykes!'

'Truly – very upsetting,' said the king, looking around desperately for his guards, who were determinedly doing their guarding from *outside* the room. After all, they had children too.

Tassie was listening to the conversation with growing fascination. Maybe she wasn't the only one who would stand up to Brutus after all . . .

'I mean,' ground on Bilge, still hypnotised by the quail, 'little rascals they might be an' I'm not denyin' it, but we invested a lot o' time and effort into bringin' 'em up, and there's been many a sacrifice to keep 'em healthy enough for a fourteen-hour-day in the fields. AND they're s'posed to look after us in our old age.'

'You're twenty-eight, Bilge!' said the king, 'Hardly retirement age!'

'Prince William says I'm undernourished. And I've got rickets.'

The king gave a forced laugh. 'Well, we're ALL undernourished and have rickets, Bilge!' he said heartily, stifling a burp. 'It doesn't mean that we can just lie down and let someone else do the work, does it? It's the duty of every man, woman and child in the kingdom to carry their weight and strive for the good of us all. Minchett!' he bellowed over his shoulder. 'You can clear the table now!'

'That's as maybe,' said Bilge, turning his peasant hat in his hands, 'and I'm sure yer Kingship is right, but I mus' warn you that folks is mighty upset about the joust tomorrer. Prince Billy is a popular chap around the hovels. Always a kind word for the lepers, and very quick with 'is money for beggars. And folk around here just don't take to knights with pointy beards who sell their children.'

The king rose, and began to slide off towards the side door.

'Well, it's good of you to come, Bilge. Rest assured, I shall be having a chat with my dear nephew from Badspite. As a token of my gratitude to the twelve of you, please take this small quail. Goodnight.' And he showed a clean and speedy pair of heels as the Bilges closed in on the plate.

Over near the door, Tassie gave Gramma a little kick towards the group.

'You just need to ask, you know,' said Gramma testily.

'Sorry, I forgot.'

'Yes, well, I might forget and put you through a slit window next time,' murmured Gramma.

'What does Bilge do?' asked Tassie, as they approached.

'He's a reaper,' said Gramma. 'Fastest scythe in the province when he puts his mind to it. The horses love him because he brings the hay.'

'*Really*?' mused Tassie. 'That's most interestin'. Mr Bilge!' she called. 'Can I have a word, please?'

Bilge turned around, thumbing the last quail feathers into his mouth. In his world, people with tops that sparkled and horses parked under their bottoms, even indoors, were obviously very important. So he knuckled his forehead respectfully.

'Yes . . . er . . . master?' he said, eyeing the jeans. 'Or . . . ma'am, yer ladyship . . . ,' he guessed, seeing the pink trainers. 'Can I be of h'assistance?'

Tassie gave a big smile, and leapt lightly from the

saddle. She felt she was getting the hang of this riding malarkey.

'Bilge!' she said, taking his arm. 'Mrs Bilge!' she said, linking hers. 'I think actually it might be *me* that can help *you*!'

'Well, bless me soul,' said Mrs Bilge in wonder. 'That don't 'appen often! Are you sure that's what you want?'

'Oh very much,' said Tassie. 'You see, I've got this plan . . .'

It was after midnight when the knock came on Violetzka's door. Without even waking up properly, Violetzka muttered one of her Mazovian curses and threw a chamber pot at the door. There was some frantic whispering, and then came another knock, a little louder this time.

'Mistress Violetzka! Can we come in? Er . . . are you unarmed?'

'By Siegred and ze Seven Silver Slabs of Cake!' exclaimed Violetzka, yawning and striding over to the door. 'I tell you, if zere isn't one, ze darningest goot reason for zis and two, also anozzer goot reason, neither of vich have anyzing to do viz roses, zen you'd better have ze vorld's greatest running slippers on . . . oh!'

Two of the Bilge brood blinked up at her in the

candlelight like frightened fledgelings.

'Be this a rose?' asked one, nervously, taking a single rambler out from behind his back.

'Grrrrr!' said Violetzka, on a rising scale.

'Tassie sent it. Said it were a joke!' squeaked the younger boy with the sores, cowering.

Violetzka pulled them into the room and closed the door. 'That little mizzy is going to get her bottom spankered ven I am Queen,' she grumbled, but her eyes were shining and eager. 'Vere is she? She vanished – puff – from ze rope! Is zere word of my love, my Billee?'

The Bilges stared around the room with their jaws flapping on the floor. Their whole lane wasn't as big as this! The bed could have slept three families without a fight, and they couldn't spot an open sewer anywhere.

'Boys – an answer please!' Violetzka snapped her fingers to regain their attention.

'Oh. Um. Miss Tassie, she says would you scoo . . . scutt . . .'

'Scootle,' said Germlin, the younger of the boys. 'She said scootle.'

'Scootle. Could you scootle down to the Banqueting Hall with us for a council of wire?' finished Arthur Bilge proudly.

'Hm. And you are sure she said "wire"?'

Arthur screwed up his face and thought. 'Could'a been "war",' he admitted eventually.

Violetzka clapped her hands together girlishly. The thunderclouds left her face and the sun came shining through. She seized the boys by the hands and ran to the door.

'Come on zen!' she cried gaily. 'Quickly now!'

'Oh. An' Tassie, she said can ye bring the roses, m'lady?'

The smile froze on the princess's face. 'All of zem?' she whispered hoarsely.

It was some time later that the three of them wheeled the four-poster bed into the passageway, festooned with roses of each and every sort. Germlin was positioned on the front, hanging on to a post, to shout directions. Violetzka, a little short-tempered after tangling with a million thorns, took a deep breath.

'Right!' she said. 'Lead ze vay. You do *know* ze vay, don't you?'

'Yes mistress, right mistress,' said Arthur. He hailed his brother. 'Germlin boy, just follow all the breadcrumbs I dropped on the way up 'ere and us'll be back in two twitches!'

There was a long silence in the front. 'Breadcrumbs?' quavered Germlin.

'Aar. All the breadcrumbs Tassie gave me to drop. Follow 'em back to the hall.'

Silence.

'Germlin,' said Arthur after a moment. 'You ate 'em, didn't you?'

And Germlin started to cry.

Chapter 15

S trange things happened on the night before the joust at Huffington Castle. Guards kept being woken up by odd sounds and whisperings. Once they'd discovered that the noises came from Tassie, as she scurried around getting her plans in place, they just pulled their helmets down lower over their eyes and hummed loudly, pretending that nothing was happening. The 'scary hair' incident was still fresh in their minds.

The king, having finally got off to sleep despite a total lack of bed sheets, found himself rudely prodded awake in the wee small hours.

'Wha . . . wha . . . what?' he cried out blindly, wondering if the peasants were revolting.

'Jus' checkin',' said a familiar voice in the dark.

'Are you goin' to stop this fight or not?'

'What? Godsplut and Fie madam, certainly not! Get out of my room!'

'Final answer?'

'NO!' roared the king. 'The Huffington honour shall not be betrayed! I'm a king you know!'

'I know you're a silly old fart!' said Tassie, and slipped out of the room while the king lashed about, trying to light his candle. When eventually he managed it, he stuck his head out angrily into the corridor. A peculiar squeaking noise was coming from the adjoining passage at the far end. As the king watched incredulously, a four-poster bed covered in roses sailed slowly past, guided by a small boy with a flaming torch. The king scurried back to bed and pulled straw over his head.

Tassie trotted on through a maze of passageways, wishing she'd brought Gramma along to give her a ride. Eventually she came upon the Bilges she'd put on Brutus Duty, to make sure the bully wasn't up making mischief. Hearing nothing from Brutus's room for a while, Harry Bilge had tied a thread around the iron door latch, laying it out down the passage and round a corner, where he wound the other end around his big toe.

'Jus' like poachin',' whispered Harry to Tassie, as he settled his sleepy little sister down next to him. 'Us'll know if we gets a bite! By the by, Brutus is 'avin' a right ol' rage. 'E 'ad to be cut from 'is armour after you gave 'im that there bashin'!'

Tassie snorted with laughter. 'Like corned beef from a tin,' she chortled.

'What?' asked Harry.

'Never mind,' said Tassie. 'I'm off to meet Princess Violetzka in the Banqueting Hall.'

But Violetzka and her crew, after what seemed a lifetime lost in the passages of the castle, had finally reached the end of their tether. Germlin's torch sputtered and went out.

'BUZZARDS!' shouted Violetzka, and sat down

on the footboard for a sulk. Unfortunately, the bed was only a few inches away from the top of the king's staircase, and the movement tipped them over the edge.

'Eeeeeeeeeeeee!' screamed the Bilges in unison as they plummeted into the darkness, faces lashed by flying rose stems.

'Uh-uh-uh-uh-uh-uh-uh . . .' commented Violetzka, as they jolted down a seemingly endless flight of stairs.

'Oops!' said Tassie, just before the bed scooped her up off the steps and ploughed onwards down the black stairwell.

Hanging on grimly, they saw the twinkling lights of the Banqueting Hall just moments before they hit the floor. The bed careered across the full length of the room at top speed. It was Gramma, searching for leftovers on the banqueting table, who saved the day. Hearing the sound of what could only be a runaway four-poster bed, she strolled over to the great double doors of the entrance and kicked them wide open.

The bed whooshed out, through the courtyard,

across the drawbridge and into the night. It hit the kitchen rubbish tip at full throttle, launched into the air . . . and slapped back to earth a good fifty metres further down the castle mound. There was a bloodcurdling scream, a mighty crunching of wood, and a final, echoing *smack* . . . the Rose Arbour had its roses back again.

'I can't believe that didn't wake the whole castle!' whispered Tassie, flat on her back in a compost heap, not daring to move.

Violetzka sat up and spat petals. 'I have ze FREEDOM!' she said, gazing around the moonlit scene as if she'd forgotten what the world looked like without stone walls. 'Vere is zat slimeveasel, Brutus? I shall show 'im vot "bad spite" is, viz all ze big brass knobs on! I shall rip ze little lumps off 'im . . .' She was up and striding back to the castle when Tassie brought her down by the ankle.

'No!' she said firmly. 'Not right now. For one thing, it wouldn't be sportin'.'

'Vot?' said Violetzka incredulously. 'Sportink?'

'Well, he's prob'ly asleep, and he hasn't got his big brave armour on, and you're a girl and he's just a lousy bully. He wouldn't stand a chance. Some people might say that you were kickin' a man when he was down.'

'Ya, ze kicking, and ze fingers poking in ze eyes also . . .' Violetzka struggled to free her ankle.

'Come on Violetzka, that's not goin' to work. What about our Billy? How will he feel if you fight his battles for him? You know how much he thinks of his honour, even if he's a bit rubbish on how to defend it. If there's goin' to be any manly rough stuff, it has to be Billy that does it.'

Blimey, Tassie thought, that doesn't sound like a good idea, even to me!

Violetzka covered her eyes. 'Oh no!' she sobbed. 'Perhaps I should practise being ze Lady Badspite after all.'

Tassie spun round to stare at her.

'That's it!' she cried, an idea bursting into her mind. 'Absolutely you should! There's no point in backin' a loser after all.'

Violetzka shot her a venomous look.

'No, really,' said Tassie, her eyes starting to glint in the moonlight. 'I think it would make sense for you to stop worryin' about Billy, and start lookin' after your own future. C'mon, let's go back to the castle and talk about it. Leave the roses – we'll fetch 'em tomorrow.'

She grabbed the reluctant Violetzka's hand and the two of them began to haul each other back up the shadowy path. The sleepy cawing from disturbed rooks reminded Tassie of when she had arrived at Huffington. It seemed like a hundred years ago, rather than several hundred years in the future.

From behind them came a little mewing sound.

'Help! I've been eaten by a bed!' whimpered Germlin. 'Please get me out.'

'And so what I'm thinkin' is,' announced Tassie, striding up and down on the polished oak table in the Banqueting Hall, dripping wax from her helmet and watched by a small, tired audience of peasants and castle folk, 'that perhaps we've misunderstood Brutus.'

'*What*?' The audience buzzed with confusion, and Tassie held up her hand for silence. She put it down . . . (buzz) . . . then held it up again . . . (silence). Now *that* was power! She took a deep breath.

'I mean, Brutus is a young bloke, on his own, a long way from home. He's prob'ly lonely, and he doesn't understand any of the Huffington customs.'

'That's cos we don't 'ave a custom where you sets fire to someone's 'ouse, and sees 'ow long you can keeps 'em in it!' said someone.

'Leaky muck-tubbers!' agreed the Head Cook, juggling three meat cleavers in one hand.

'Are you sayin' us should *support* 'im?' asked Mrs Bilge disbelievingly. 'After all 'e done to us? And to our Billy? And wharrabout yer plan then? Does we give that up and all?'

Tassie folded her hands and gave her very best version of a small sugary angel. 'All I'm *sayin'* is that it wouldn't be at all *surprisin'* if people wanted to keep on the right side of the obvious winner. Of course everyone wants to make a good impression, and

153

show him how welcome he is! I jus' hope –' here Tassie shook her head and put on a worried face – 'that it's not all too much for the poor feller. After all, he's not used to trustin' people, and we might *unnerve* him and make him drop his guard. It would be a shame if he was suspicious and uncomfortable on such an important day.'

Her audience stared. They looked at each other. They looked back at Tassie.

'I thinks yer off yer tiny bonce,' said Bilge firmly.

There was a loud 'Duh!' from the middle of the crowd, and Violetzka fought her way up on to the table next to Tassie, eyes flashing and fists on hips.

'Zis plan, it is sooo peasy!' she cried, even though she'd only just got it. 'Ve give ze uckly bully all ze cheers and ze rah rahs, and he zinks we are ze pushover! His guard is droppered! And my Billee . . .'

'We make Billy angry so he *wants* to fight,' finished Tassie grimly. 'That's the tough bit.'

'Oh, ARRR!' said the castle folk, nodding and grinning at last.

A perfectly dressed servant standing slightly apart from the group, with his nose held high, raised a finger silently.

'Might I be so bold as to offer my assistance to the Young Master?' he said smoothly. 'I am Lubbers, His Highness's manservant since he was born. I believe you can rely on me to know what goes on in Sire's head.'

'Really?' asked Tassie, liking the look of the new recruit. 'Jus' how much does go on in there would you say?'

Lubbers gave a whisper of a smile. 'Madam, I could not say it is the busiest highway, but it does lead to the most noble places. I shall do my best to help.' And he nodded and left the room.

'What in the name of Good St Dingle's Armoured Pants is going on here?' growled the king, towering in the other doorway, looking very tired and cross. 'It's nearly dawn and you're making nasty marks on my best furniture. Now will you all get lost!'

He paused for a minute. 'Anyone got any bed sheets?' he asked hopefully as they filed out. 'I am the king you know!' he roared after them, but they'd disappeared.

Tassie waited until it was quiet and the king had grumped off to bed again. Then she took off her trainers and managed to skid almost the entire length of the oak table in her socks.

Chapter 16

There was just a tiny fingernail of sun sneaking up on the horizon, and most birds hadn't even *started* to think about early worms, when the Tentmaker arrived with his men in a field just outside the castle moat.

'Ginger, you get the carts unloaded. Tapwick, pace out the width we need for the Pavilion. Undersmudge, check all the poles are numbered. I'm not having the same fiasco we had at the Duke of Bellybudger's mudwrestling tournament last month. People are still laughing in three provinces.'

The Tentmaker was a tall, pompous man, as thin as one of his own poles – and you could hang your coat on his nose too.

The men jumped down off the carts and began to mill about purposefully.

'Hello,' said Tassie, sitting patiently on a tree stump in the half-light.

The Tentmaker jumped.

'S'truth! Who, by all that's holy, are you? Does your mother know you're out at this time in the morning?'

'Mm,' said Tassie noncommittally, 'the king sent me to meet you.'

'Did he? Don't see why. I've got all the instructions I need in the order he made. Let's see now. "One large pavilion tent with pointy trim. Two stripy changing tents for the contestants. One mead tent with trestle bar . . . " '

'Yes,' said Tassie, 'but they're not goin' in this field.'

'They're not?' The Tentmaker looked around. The sun had spilled over the top of the horizon now and was pouring through the fields in golden rivers. 'But this is where it said on the order. And look, the grass has been cut for us.'

'Well, the king has changed his mind. He is the king after all. His wizard told him this was an unlucky field for joustin'.'

'I don't think any field shall be lucky for Prince Billy, from what I hear,' smirked the Tentmaker.

'Maybe,' said Tassie, fixing him with a disapproving eye, 'but the field that you're after is the one over there.' And she pointed just over the ditch.

'You are snapping my garters, lady!' said the Tentmaker in horror, surveying the waist-high stinging nettles and wild grass that stretched away into the distance.

'Certainly not. The runes say that it is a lucky field, and that's the one the king wants. Bilge will cut you space for the tents.'

'And where, pray, is Bilge?' asked the Tentmaker, putting his knuckles on his hips and looking fed up.

'Right 'ere,' said a voice behind him, making him jump again. With a ten-foot scythe in one hand and the sun behind him, Bilge looked more like the Grim Reaper than a champion grass cutter. The Tentmaker made an effort to recover himself.

'Yes, well,' he said, eyeing the scythe nervously. 'Let's get on with it shall we? I want this cracked in an hour. I've got a Heathen Party at Crusade Headquarters this afternoon, and the camel-hide tents still need hemming.'

'Arr,' nodded Bilge, and strode off past him with a flourish of the scythe that nearly scalped the Tentmaker.

'Marvellous,' murmured Tassie as she watched them start work.

'Disaster!' shouted the king an hour and a half later, as he surveyed the scene. 'Is the Tentmaker a complete horse's bottom? Didn't he notice the big difference between a beautifully mown jousting field and a solid wall of horticulture? Well, let's see how good he is at pitching tents with his head pushed down a privy!'

That reminded Tassie of her family, still waiting, huddled in the turret room.

'I think I'll go and . . . um . . . see how Billy's gettin' on,' she said, edging away.

'What about my field?' moaned the king, waving at it pathetically. He made a dejected sight, standing there in a medieval dressing-gown, with knobbly bare knees and armoured boots underneath. 'I've got several hundred friends and relatives turning up in two hours for a festival of fun and excitement. Billy and Brutus couldn't find each other with a map in this lot!'

'Don't worry,' said Tassie airily. 'I've asked Bilge to sort it out. It'll be fine.'

'All right,' grumbled the king. 'I hope you know what you're doing though. It's tough enough being king without having people laughing at your tournaments.' He strode back up the hill, kicking stones and muttering, 'It's not fair.'

Tassie wondered how Gramma was getting on. She'd gone off to get some rest and at least one square meal before the Challenge. Gramma said two square meals would probably be better.

People were beginning to arrive at the field in dribs and drabs as Tassie went to follow the king. She'd never seen such a strange collection of characters before, and while she knew it was rude to stare, you'd really have to be blind or the Pope to resist the temptation here.

These, she realised, were carnival folk. Long, tall, short and round, they came: men eating fire and juggling children, women with beards and dancing on horses. A thin, ragged youth who looked like he hadn't slept for a hundred years went by, dragged behind a crazed-looking bear on a chain.

'Blimey,' said Tassie under her breath, 'what a weird bunch!'

'Hah!' replied the boy, without slowing down. 'You might think we're odd, but you be the one with a candle on your 'ead.'

'Oh yes. Thank you.' Tassie reached up and snapped it loose as she turned back to the castle. She couldn't help a slight worry. She could feel Time tugging at her, but she knew she couldn't allow it to push her out of the Middle Ages until Billy had either sunk or swum at the Challenge.

'It's only a flippin' Balloon!' she told herself sternly. 'It's not the boss of you!'

She took a deep breath and scrambled back up the path towards the castle. There was a light summer mist around the lower half of the stone walls, while the battlements and towers were bathed in early golden sunshine. Tassie thought it looked magical.

'Hmmph!' she said to herself. 'If only it were. That would save a piggin' lot of trouble!'

Inside the cool walls, the castle was beginning to awaken. The sentries were stretching and yawning, and trying to pretend that they wouldn't have slept right through an enemy invasion. Tassie gave them all a friendly wave as she passed by, which made them back off nervously.

She found Billy quite easily. Tumbledown Tower, his new quarters, was well named. It was outside the main castle, and only joined to the rest by a crumbling arched bridge, under which a gaggle of large and mean-looking bats swung gently to and fro, and occasionally plummeted into the moat when the brickwork crumbled as they slept. Even a mountain goat would have thought twice about crossing it.

Tassie took in little of this as she scuffed her way across the bridge, sidestepping a couple of lethal potholes without even noticing. She was very worried about how Billy was going to cope with the day's events. In her heart she knew that anyone who'd stick an otter down his armour for its own safety had a lot of steel about him. But Billy was in for a tough time and she hoped he could take it.

'Do come in!' came his cheery voice when she knocked at the ramshackle door. Tassie did. As soon as she walked through the arch, the Balloon of Time leapt on her, making her guts spin and the Middle Ages wobble in front of her eyes. But there was no way Tassie was leaving now!

'Hi Billy!' she said with loud determination. The wobble vanished. Her stomach settled.

Billy was sitting on the end of his bed, dressed in a long silk nightshirt and some woolly bed socks.

'Oh. Hello.' He said it cheerily enough, but then went back to drumming his fingers on his knees and staring straight ahead.

'What's wrong?' asked Tassie with concern.

'Oh nothing! Nothing at all, old thing! Nothing

wrong. No wrongness anywhere in Tumbleweed Tower. Nothing amiss or . . .' He trailed off. 'Haven't seen my manservant have you, old fruit? Only he didn't show up for work this morning for the first time ever, and I can't seem to remember what comes next in this "getting dressed" nonsense.'

Tassie smothered a laugh.

'Mm, right. Well, I can help if you like. It's not tricky once you get the hang of it. Try puttin' your outer clothes on last. It's so annoying when you've got your coat all buttoned up and you suddenly discover a vest left over. Where are your clothes?'

Billy thought carefully.

'Nope. No idea,' he said eventually. 'Lubbers normally magicks them out of somewhere. Very clever chap is Lubbers. He can tie bows too.'

'Really?' said Tassie, looking around. 'Have you got any cupboards?'

'Cupboards?' said Billy slowly, trying out the word. 'Couldn't tell you. Try looking in that box thing on legs over there.'

'What, this cupboard?' muttered Tassie, throwing it open.

'Oh jolly well done!' cheered Billy, recognising some items. He jumped to his feet eagerly. 'Look, if you could possibly lay 'em out in the right order, I think I can crack this.'

Tassie wasn't terribly sure what the right order was in the 'Olden Days', but she had a good guess and left Billy behind a tapestry screen to get changed.

'Shouldn't you shower first?' she asked, strolling over to the window to look out.

'Shower?'

'Yes . . . wash, soap, flannel . . . you know.'

'In August?' Billy laughed. 'I'm an October chap myself. Anyway, I'm rather thinking of having myself scraped. Apparently they swore by it in ancient Rome. Rather good for getting the goose fat off your skin when winter ends I should imagine.'

Tassie shuddered.

'I'll have to talk it over with Lubbers,' Billy chatted on. 'He's jolly up on that sort of thing, and really he is in charge of looking after my royal person. The outside bit anyway. (What's this? Does that go on my . . .? No, doesn't seem to. Perhaps if I just stick it on my head for now . . .) *You* don't happen to know where Lubbers is do you? I'm a bit worried about him. He's such a faithful and loyal soul and he wouldn't let me down if his life depended on it, bless him.'

Tassie was looking out of the window.

'Er, yes, I do know where he is,' she said carefully. 'He's down in the courtyard with all the other servants, givin' Brutus a hero's welcome.'

There was a silence so loud, it made Tassie want to cover her ears. It seemed to go for an awfully long time. She couldn't bear to watch as Billy appeared very slowly around one side of the screen, looking almost like he was sleepwalking, dragging one foot after another over to the window to stand next to Tassie.

The gates of the castle had been thrown wide open, and even from their isolated tower, they could see the large crowd of servants that had gathered in the courtyard. On the breeze came the sound of frenzied cheering as Brutus appeared at his window. Billy and Tassie watched wordlessly as he peered down at the throng. He looked behind him uncertainly. Then he leant out and tried to look up at the battlements above him. Finally he seemed to realise that the crowd really was cheering *him*, and he raised his arms in a royal wave. Hats went into the air. Then he clasped his hands together above his head like a champion. The crowd went wild. Dancing broke out, and something that looked like an early Mexican wave.

'Oh,' said Billy quietly. 'They seem to rather like the old cuz, don't they?'

Tassie thought her heart was going to break. She gritted her teeth.

Billy turned to her and forced a ragged smile. 'Well, that's marvellous, isn't it? I mean, there was never really a chance that I would win today, was there? And it's very important that a new heir is popular with his people. It looks like I'll be leaving the kingdom in safe hands. Good-o.'

Tassie almost smacked her forehead with frustration.

This was not the reaction she had been hoping for!

Just what, she wondered wildly, did it take to make this boy lose his temper? Whatever it was, she had to find it fast. She rounded on Billy, and drew a deep, deep breath.

'Oh yeah, right!' she shouted into his surprised face. 'And I s'pose you think that lets you off the hook, do you?'

'Wha . . . what?' Billy staggered back, as if suddenly savaged by a favourite kitten. Tassie was straight after him with a wagging finger dangerously close to his nose.

'Very noble, I'm sure!' she mocked. ' "Oh the people all love him so I'll jus' lay down and die and everyone else'll live happily ever after!" Shows how much you know, Mr Smarty-Tights!'

'But they do love him! Look down there. All that cheering and shouting and hat-chucking and stuff. It would be much better if I just got out of the way.' Billy was still on the retreat, and trying to hide behind a low table.

But by now, Tassie had worked herself up into a

right old fury, and was rather enjoying the experience. She jumped up on a handy chair so she could grab Billy by the front of his tunic and stick her nose millimetres from his.

'Listen, you lanky streak of custard,' she snarled. 'If someone was threatenin' to sell *your* children, *you'd* try and get on the right side of them, wouldn't you?'

Billy's jaw dropped about a foot. He looked completely aghast.

'But . . . but . . . that's not *allowed*!' he sputtered.

'Not jus' now maybe, but it will be by the time we're collectin' bits of you off the jousting field! Why don't you ask the Bilges? Brutus has got offers on most of their kids.' She flung out an arm towards the window. 'There's Mrs Bilge – near the front of the crowd, wavin' till her little hands drop off. And they're not the only ones!'

Billy almost collapsed on to the chair behind him, but Tassie hadn't let go of his tunic.

'Oh yes. *You* might be happily out of the way, but what about the serfs and the servants that he kicks all over the castle? Or your King Pa when he gets in the way, which will be by about lunchtime tomorrow I should think?' Tassie shook the tunic like a terrier with a rat. 'So, "Mr S'cuse Me While I Pop Off and Die", where does that leave your clever little scheme now? Huh? Huh?' She checked the chair was still behind him, and dropped him in it with a thump.

Billy just sat there, slumped over, his head in his hands. Tassie had to grip her own hands behind her back to stop herself from at least patting him on the head. She waited, fists clenched, breathing all but stopped. And she waited. And she waited. If she lost him now, there was nothing more she could do for him, or Huffington, or the miserable generations that would suffer down the years.

'I'm not having that.' His voice was so low, it could have been her own imagination. But then Billy looked up. His big blue eyes had lost their mild, slightly goofy look, and he was straightening up in his chair as if someone was pumping air into his back at a rate of knots.

'I'm not having that!' he repeated loudly in a voice like steel, and stood up. 'I WON'T let him sell the children!'

'AND he's given Violetzka a wedding date,' said Tassie, to crank up the pressure. It was only a teeny lie.

'No, by all the Hair Puddings on Hell's Table!' shouted Billy. 'He will NOT marry my bride! Where is my armour? Where is my sword?' He began to stride boldly around his quarters, not even noticing when he broke furniture. 'I will teach the Bad Smell of Badspite a few manners before the day is out! If Brutus triumphs in the end, it will not be through any fault of mine!'

'Well,' said Tassie, with satisfaction, 'I've got some things to do. I'll find Lubbers and send him up.'

'By the way,' she added, 'the drawers go under your tights, not on your head.'

Brutus hadn't slept very well. When he did nod off, it was only to relive that last wild charge across the courtyard and the world turning upside down as he got stuck on the end of Tassie's lance. Not to mention the really nasty bit where his head tangled with the ground and the ground won. This might have made a less dedicated villain think about all the unfortunates he'd spiked over the years, but it only made Brutus so angry that he'd ground his teeth almost smooth overnight.

He'd also been disturbed in the wee small hours by strange rumbling noises, exactly like a four-poster bed being driven aimlessly round the corridors. And when he'd finally got up to see what was happening, he'd flung open the door furiously, only to discover a ten-year-old boy hopping up and down and screaming that his toe was broken. It was very off-putting.

And if all that wasn't enough, suddenly this morning, everyone seemed to like him! Brutus couldn't remember the last time anyone had looked him in the eye and smiled. Gibbered, maybe. Wept, of course, but never *smiled*. First of all it was the boy bringing his spiced milk in bed. (He looked rather familiar, and had a bandage around the end of his foot.) He wore an expression that made Brutus think he had a painful toothache, but then he suddenly realised the lad was grinning at him!

'What?' Brutus had growled, wondering if he had bed-hair.

'Just wantin' to wish you all the very best, Sire,' said Harry Bilge, putting the milk down on the bedside table, 'Us are rootin' for you, Sire, me and the stable boys. And the kitchen maids.'

'Really?' Brutus didn't care for this game one little bit.

'Oh yes, Sire. We got this little song. You know, for

when yer joustin'. To sort of encourage you like. Ahem.'
He began to recite in a reedy voice:

> *'He's Brutus of Badspite, he's mean and he's bad,*
> *His hair is all spiky, and folks say he's mad,*
> *He's cruel and he's nasty, his breath makes you wince,*
> *But we all love him cos he's our new prince!'*

'What think you Sire? Sung to the tune o' "Follow the Master and Cobble 'is Spuds", a Harvest Time favourite, Sire . . . sir.'

'Come here,' said Brutus. The boy shuffled closer, still smiling. Brutus picked up the sword he kept under the bed and delivered an almighty thwack to the lad's backside with the flat of the blade. He picked up his milk and lay back in bed.

'Write a song about that,' he grunted. 'Now get lost.'

'Yes, Sire, thank you, Sire. Crossin' my fingers, Sire!' the boy bobbed a quick bow and disappeared, rubbing his bottom.

★

It was while he was sipping his milk and imagining Billy's head on a spike that Brutus heard some strange noises down in the courtyard. It was still only early, so he hopped out of bed, meaning to tear a few strips off whoever was disturbing his rest.

The roar that greeted his appearance at the window nearly sent him under the bed with fright. Like all bullies, he wasn't as brave as he was nasty. But just as he turned to run, he noticed something odd. Everyone was waving at him! And they were all smiling too. Some of them were shouting out things like 'Good luck!' and 'Huzzah!' and even 'Go Brutus!'

'That's strange,' thought Brutus, looking behind him to see if someone else called Brutus had walked in without him noticing.

'They almost seem to . . . like me!' he was forced to think, but that didn't sound right, so he leant out and had a good look around the battlements to make sure it wasn't someone else they were cheering. No. He was definitely the toast of the town. A small, savage smile crawled across his face.

'The poor fools,' he said to himself, and gave a royal sort of wave that caused the crowd to erupt with joy. 'The stupid, pathetic, creeping, miserable wretches,' he chuckled under his breath. He clenched his hands above his head like a champion, and couldn't believe it when people started actually dancing. 'Don't they know what I have in store for them, the imbeciles?'

'I can't believe 'e's fallin' for all this,' whispered a peasant, swinging his wife round by the arm and waving at Brutus's window like a village idiot. ''E must think we don't know what 'e's got in store for us, the dip'ead.'

'Hee hee hee!' chortled Brutus, rubbing his hands together as he turned away from the window. 'Billy's not going to like this!' He did a delighted little jig around the room.

'Would you be wantin' to break yer fast now, Sire?' asked Harry Bilge, who had quietly re-entered the room and was watching him with interest.

Brutus stumbled in mid-pirouette, went a deep

aubergine colour and rounded on the boy.

'Yes!' he shouted, because he was, after all, hungry. 'Get out of my sight and call me when it's ready. And where's my manservant? I need to get dressed.' He aimed another hefty kick at Harry's behind, but a Bilge doesn't get caught on the hop twice (not even with a broken toe), and Brutus's bare foot caught the closing door with a crack that made his eyes water.

Chapter 18

Back in the Banqueting Hall, the king was stomping around, still in his dressing gown. Since Tassie last saw him down in the fields, he seemed to have slipped from 'unhappy' to 'apoplectic' without even changing gear at 'furious'.

'Hi king. Wassup?' Tassie greeted him cheerfully, as at least half her plan was ticking along nicely.

The king glared at her.

'You're not going to believe this,' he said, clearly because he didn't. 'We've been invaded!'

'Really?' said Tassie, concerned. 'Er, how badly?'

'As badly as it gets, madam!' roared the king. 'A whole family has moved in to one of my castle rooms and refuses to leave! I'll have their heads for this!'

'I see,' said Tassie uneasily. 'And what room would that be exactly?'

'One of the privies. Would you believe it?' The king shook his head wildly. 'Bod's Bunions! It's outrageously unchivalrous and I forbid it. I absolutely forbid it!'

'You can't forbid it, it's already happened. Don't you have your own privy?' Tassie tried to swallow her sudden panic. Her family had crossed the centuries!

'Of course, but the servants are de-lousing the Royal Apartments and I can't even get in the door! And I'm certainly not walking half a mile to the guest wing. Even if I could find it.' He crossed his arms and sulked. 'It's MY castle, and I'll use whichever garderobe I like. So there.'

'Mm. What are you goin' to do?' asked Tassie, her mind whirring like an over-wound clock. She wondered what her family had made of being discovered by a giant king in his dressing gown. Oh, and of being in the thirteenth century of course – if they'd noticed.

'I'll send up the guards. They can winkle them out with pikes and swords. I'm surprised they didn't choose a different room anyway. It's a bit small for a family.'

'I expect it was the "convenience",' said Tassie. 'He he.'

The king glared. 'If you haven't got anything useful to say, I suggest you disappear.'

'As it happens, I have,' said Tassie brightly. 'I would say that you should let them stew in their own juice for the day – if you'll pardon the expression. After all, you don't need the hassle right now. And what are they goin' to do, locked in a privy? I'd wait until you have a bit of time when you can *really* show them how angry you are.'

The king harrumphed sulkily, but he did rather like the idea of clapping the invaders in irons and giving them a long, stern lecture on knightly conduct.

'And you should get a wriggle on if you don't want to be late for your guests.' Tassie was ushering him out of the hall like a soothing shepherd with a cranky sheep. 'Why don't you jus' leave it to me, while you get ready?'

The king allowed himself a sudden grin.

'Madam, you are a diplomat, and a politician.

I could do with a son like you. At the moment I'd settle for one who could hold a lance at the horizontal,' he finished under his breath.

'Look, what did I tell you? Don't come out, and don't let anyone in,' hissed Tassie through the privy keyhole, thirty seconds later. 'Now open this door.'

'Well, make your mind up!' said her mother crossly as the lock clicked. 'And where have you been? What's happening downstairs? Is that Spotty Guide still there? Can you find us some tea? What have you done to your clothes? Where did you get that helmet? Why have you got wax on your shoulders . . .?'

'Muuu . . . uum!' screamed Tassie, reeling under the flood of questions. 'Everythin's fine . . .'

'Is it?' broke in her father, glaring. 'I have a medieval toilet stuck to my bottom. Lil drank her way through a family-pack of Ribena earlier and is now crossing her legs and trying not to think about waterfalls *because* I have a medieval toilet stuck to my bottom. My family is being threatened by a pimply axeman who is clearly insane, and the signal has gone on the mobile. And that's fine, is it?'

'And there was some absolutely *awful* man who opened the door earlier, wearing a grotty horsehair dressing gown and a crown. He was extremely rude in front of the Twins!' said Tassie's mum.

The Twins grinned happily.

'Mummy says he must have been one of those historical actors, like the ones that tried to set fire to me last time,' said Lil importantly. 'She said he could take his crown and stick it . . .'

'Thank you, Lil, that'll do!' said Mrs Ripley primly. 'I've told you not to listen when Mummy's talking to bad people.'

'Don't worry about him,' said Tassie. 'That's jus' . . . er . . . Mr King. He's havin' a bad day.'

'Ordering us about like he owned the place!' snorted Mrs Ripley. 'I'll be writing to the National Trust.'

'Yes, well, I think there *is* a family connection,' said Tassie vaguely. 'Now, the police are startin' to get things under control downstairs, so if you can just wait here a little longer . . .'

'As if I had a choice,' grumbled her father.

'. . . I'll come and get you when the coast is clear,' said Tassie.

Mrs Ripley peered over her shoulder. 'And what have you done with Gramma? Is she OK?'

'Oh yes, she's in a stable.'

The Ripleys stared.

'Er . . . in a stable *condition*. You know. Totally cool,' finished Tassie, trying to back away. 'Lock the door behind me, won't you?' And she quickly slammed it shut on four different questions.

Chapter 19

The courtyard was absolutely jam-packed with people by the time Tassie emerged into the sunshine. She stopped on the stone step, and stared about her in awe. A troupe of tumbling dwarfs flip-flapped past her nose and on around the yard, scattering laughing lords and ladies. A fire-eater was sending great gobs of flame up into the blue sky, to the anxiety of the castle pigeons, and there was an almost solid smell of singed hair and roasting meat and, naturally, body odour.

It was so colourful and bizarre, Tassie wished she had a camera. Through the open gates she could see a great trail of more folk, summoned from all over the tiny kingdom and further afield to witness the famous joust. Every road to Huffington was alive with people on the move. There were quite a few Badspitians, swaggering through the crowd and kicking the locals out of the way as if they owned the place. Of the Huffs, many were toffs, noticed Tassie sourly, who were anxious to meet the new prince and put in a good word for themselves. But there were a lot of peasants too. Peasants who were really fond of Prince Billy, because he wasn't like the others. They weren't very clever, because the toffs didn't let them get clever, and they weren't very brave, because mostly their masters beat that out of them, but they wanted to help, and Tassie thought their children might have some fight in them. Even though she knew Billy was still in terrible danger, she felt a bit better. Then she caught sight of Billy's manservant, Lubbers, like a perfectly dressed iceberg, sailing disdainfully through the tide of people and keeping his nose well above armpit level.

'Madam,' he said, inclining his head just a touch as he reached her. 'I trust the Plan progresses satisfactorily?'

'Buzzin'!' nodded Tassie. 'You looked very convincin', wavin' at Brutus.'

'An unpleasant duty, to pretend liking for such a low creature,' agreed Lubbers, sniffing. 'Still, anyone who has to listen to the Young Master's views on washing must soon become an accomplished actor, or resign his post. I take it "the fire is lit"?'

'He's burnin' like a box of Chinese crackers,' said Tassie happily. 'D'you know? I think he could almost beat Brutus without us interferin' any more!'

Lubbers smiled in polite disbelief. 'Madam,' he reminded her, 'I have seen His Highness's knees. They are not the knees of a warrior.'

'No, perhaps you're right. Anyway, can you wriggle up there and get him dressed properly? He needs his armour too.'

Lubbers bowed again. 'It is absolutely my pleasure, lady.' He stopped just as he squeezed past her to enter the castle, and said, 'Undergarments on the head?'

''Fraid so.'

Lubbers raised his eyes heavenward. 'Who knows where his powers might end if only he could dress himself.'

No sooner had he gone than Bilge appeared, walking up the path from the field and whistling tunelessly, with his scythe over one shoulder. He touched his forelock as he came up to Tassie.

'Right missis,' he greeted her. 'I done the job, like you said. I've cut some goodly swathes through that ol' long grass, and there's quite a few down there as are keelin' over with the sneezin' . . .'

'Brilliant . . .' said Tassie, almost rubbing her hands with glee.

'. . . and I'm sorry about the midget acrobats. I couldn't see 'em in the long grass, so some of 'em might be a bit shorter even than what they was, if you get my meaning, missis.'

'Yuck!' said Tassie. 'Oh well, not much we can do about that now. Do you think everything is ready?'

'Aar, I reckon so. Ye seen any o' me brats recently? I only seen one, and 'e were doing somethin' odd, puttin' his leg in then out, shaking his arms all about and turnin' round like an idjit!'

'Oh, good!' said Tassie, pleased. 'I taught him to

do that.' And she walked off, leaving Bilge to fret about just why she might have done that.

Tassie gave a quick cartwheel of happiness up on to the water trough and over the other side. Everything seemed to be going according to the Plan, and Billy was fired up like a Roman Candle. What, she thought to herself chirpily, could *possibly* go wrong?

'Tassie darling!' said her mother from right beside her ear, and Tassie just about had a heart attack.

Chapter 20

'But . . . what . . . how . . .?' Tassie gabbled. Her mother carried on as if she hadn't spoken.

'This is splendid, isn't it?' she asked, looking round at the courtyard scene admiringly. 'How do they do it? I keep looking out for someone in a wristwatch. That's always the giveaway on these historical films. Oh, look at the jester over there! He keeps bopping that charm-seller on the head with his pig's bladder. Isn't it amazing what they thought was amusing in the old days? Oh! The charm-seller's turned round and punched him! Well, that was a lot funnier, I must say. Haven't they hidden the cameras well?'

'Mum!' said Tassie, desperately trying to stem the flood of words. 'What are you doin' here?

You're s'posed to be locked in the toilet.' She was panic-stricken by seeing her mother in the thirteenth century. Her family always caused havoc in her own time, but it was far, far more important now that they didn't get in the way of her carefully laid plans. Billy and the whole of Huffington depended on her!

'Yes, well, we had a bit of luck freeing your father. I found a bottle of suntan oil in my handbag, and we rubbed it around –'

'Yes, yes,' said Tassie, anxious to avoid the gruesome details. 'But why did you come out? It might have been dangerous.'

'We had to! Poor Lil was absolutely desperate for the loo, but you know what she's like – nothing shifts if you watch her. So we all had to go outside and pretend we couldn't hear her. Well, Sam got a whiff of the pig-roast down here, and before we knew it he was down the stairs and crawling through people's legs. Can't you see the others? They're all queuing up with the actors. Look, there's Daddy pulling that man's beard . . . good grief! It's a woman!'

'And what are you goin' to do now?' asked Tassie nervously.

'I think we'll stay for the show,' said her mother, looking at her watch and tapping the dial with a frown. 'It can't be nearly as late as we thought it was, and all those horrid tourists seem to have gone. You don't want to go home yet, do you?' she asked.

'Oh no,' said Tassie hurriedly. 'In fact, I've been offered a part in the . . . er . . . film. Isn't that excitin'?'

'Oh yes! Very exciting! What are you going to be? A lord's daughter? A young peasant maiden?'

'Actually I'm goin' to be Prince William's squire,' said Tassie, knowing this wouldn't go down well.

'A squire!' Her mother was upset. 'It's the jeans, isn't it? And that's what you get for tucking your hair under your helmet. Couldn't we, just for once, see you in a nice dress?'

'I'm a squire,' said Tassie mutinously. 'It's a much more interestin' part. Anyway, I've got to go now. Please Mum, try not to be . . . you know . . . *obvious* around here.'

Mrs Ripley bristled. 'I'm sure I don't know what you mean,' she said. 'You know we never like to poke our noses in unless we're asked!'

'Yes, Mum,' said Tassie unhappily, watching her father explain to the pig-roaster that he was doing it wrong. 'Jus' try not to talk to anyone. They're all really into their roles, and everyone knows how moody actors get when they're workin'.'

Tassie walked off in the direction of the stables. By the time she had gone twenty paces, her mother was already deep in conversation with a swarthy knight from the Crusades. 'Really?' Tassie heard her say. 'And what did he say when you'd done that? Mm . . . mm . . . no, there's no recovering from that sort of thing they say . . .'

Once clear of the throng, Tassie ran most of the way to find Gramma. After the press of hot bodies outside, the cool, shadowy stables smelled rather nice and fresh, but Tassie was too wound up to notice.

'Gramma!' she shouted. 'Gramma! Where are you?'

'Mifflewump,' came a voice from the first stable.

Tassie peeked over the door, and saw Gramma, most of her face hidden by a large nosebag. Gramma tried again.

'Shnack,' she explained, her mouth full. 'Jusht keeping my shtrength up, like you said. I've got a ousht to . . . er . . . jousht.'

'Never mind that,' puffed Tassie, going in and pulling off the nosebag. 'They're out! They're free!'

'Who are?' asked Gramma, spraying the stable with oats like a combine harvester in full production.

'My family! They're outside in the crowd right now! They think they're watchin' a film bein' made!'

'Oh dear,' said Gramma. 'That's not good. I could lose my licence for this. The MoOD Council will have me grated and served in a chilled salad. Not that it's really my fault that they're here, but of course the Ministry won't see it that way . . .'

'Do you think they'll get in the way of the Plan?' interrupted Tassie anxiously. Her cheery confidence of earlier had taken a bashing the moment her mother had popped up.

'I'm sure everything will be fine,' said Gramma soothingly, giving Tassie's shoulder a friendly nuzzle. 'I mean, how much harm can they do?' There was a silence. 'I shouldn't have said that, should I?' she asked.

'No,' said Tassie, starting to pace around the stable, 'but there really isn't much we can do about them now. And if they think they're in a film, perhaps they might behave themselves.' She stopped pacing and lifted her foot to inspect the bottom of her shoe.

'Sorry, dear,' said Gramma, catching her expression. 'It's no good looking at me like that. They don't house-train horses you know!'

Tassie grabbed a handful of hay for a mopping-up operation. 'I don't suppose,' she said, 'there's any way you could swap places with Brutus's horse, is there? I mean, if Brutus was ridin' you, we've pretty much got him where we want him, haven't we?'

'I've already been down that road,' Gramma said, 'and there were three things that put me off. The first is that Brutus might just notice that his horse had been switched, his horse being black as a mineshaft and me being pure white. The second is that Brutus wears spurs the size of steak knives and there's no way he's getting on *my* back thank you. And the third is . . . well, see for yourself. That's his horse in the opposite stable. Dastard his name is. Go and say hello.'

Tassie did. Both parts of Dastard's door were firmly shut, so Tassie slipped out the rusty pin locking the upper half, opened it wide and poked her nose in. A razor-sharp hoof whistled past her ear.

'Billy couldn't get within screaming distance of that thing, let alone ride it.' Gramma said. 'In fact, it's more likely Dastard will kill Brutus than anyone else! I think he must have had a bad experience as a colt cos he's certainly very angry about something now.'

'Yes, thank you so much – not – for the warning,' said Tassie, checking her ear was still where it was meant to be. 'Oh well, I s'pose the next best thing is for you to keep Billy out of too much trouble.'

'I'll do my best,' Gramma was eyeing the nosebag

again. 'But you know what he's like. I've met frogspawn with a better seat on a horse. And if he comes out with so much as a limerick, I'm throwing him off!'

Chapter 21

Brutus had had about enough of celebrity. Just occasionally, while he was growing up, he'd wondered what it must be like to be popular – to have friends who said nice things and wished you well. Now he knew, and he was glad he hadn't wasted his time being polite to people. It was making him physically sick.

'Wassis?' he'd growled, walking into his private dining room for breakfast.

There was applause and cheering from a small crowd of grinning servants, who bobbed and bowed and nudged each other.

'Breakfast, your Greatness,' said one man, stepping forward and tugging his forelock. 'Seven courses, starting with Quick-Dry Porridge.'

'But I don't want all that!' said Brutus, eyeing it.

'Are you some sort of half-wit? How am I going to fight a challenge with that sloshing round inside me?'

The crowd looked heartbroken. Their faces dropped in disappointment.

'I'm sorry, Sire. It was made for you special like. We only wanted to show how much we supported you.' There was a sob from the back.

Brutus looked at their faces, then at the spread before him. There were pies and tarts and whole sides of bacon and ham . . .

'Well . . .' he said, weakening. It had nothing to do with the feelings of the servants around him. It was simply that he was the greediest man who'd ever set foot in the Kingdom of Huffington.

'I didn't know we was doing wrong, master,' said the man, looking downcast.

Brutus barely heard him. He'd just got a scent of the Pig's Trotter Pie, and his stomach was climbing up through his throat to reach it. 'Whatever,' he growled, and threw himself into a chair. 'Feed me.'

The crowd perked up and nodded and smiled at

each other. They bustled around, one pulling out Brutus's chair for him, and another tucking in a bib. A dozen people pressed plates on him from every direction.

Once he'd started, Brutus found it impossible to stop. Just as he licked the last crumbs from one dish, it was whisked away and another appeared in its place. It was as if the cooks were keeping one step ahead of him, frothing up yet another omelette even as Brutus was starting work on a new pie. He was like a massive locust, sweeping everything in sight into his maw, his jaws chewing and grinding endlessly. Three times he had to push his chair back as his belly grew.

'Wine!' he demanded, and a huge goblet brimming with ruby red wine was pressed into his hand. He drank like a thirsty bath plughole, washing all the food down.

Then, with great fanfare, a vast cake was brought in – drizzled with honey and nuts and made in the shape of a sword, with the Badspite crest picked out in dried fruit on the hilt.

'Made special for you, sir,' said the most senior steward. 'A little something to keep your strength up in the heat of battle, you might say.'

Brutus eyed the confection greedily. He was just about to break most of the pointy end off, when he noticed that the room had gone very quiet, and every single face was leaning in, watching him with a sort of hopeful intensity.

The penny dropped.

'No,' he said, after a moment. He leant back slowly, and tried to cross his arms over his distended belly. 'I should not make a hog of myself, should I? Tell you what,' he burped, pushing his chair back. 'I think it's time you all had a bite to eat. Seat yourselves, lads, and have some cake.'

The stewards whimpered and tried to back away.

'EAT IT!' roared Brutus, 'NOW!' He grabbed a large handful of stickiness, and shoved it in the senior steward's protesting mouth. 'And you lot – come on! Or the bloodletting begins!'

Turning several different shades of green, the

stewards sat down and ate. And whatever it was they had put in Brutus's celebration cake, they were definitely not looking forward to seeing it reappear in about half an hour's time.

'Oh Gawd!' moaned a Bilge cousin quietly as he swallowed a huge gobful, under Brutus's grinning gaze. 'There b'ain't enuff privies in the realm to cope with us lot now!'

Finally Brutus thought it was time for him to get a move on.

'Got to go,' he grunted, hauling himself to his feet and giving a mighty belch. The servants watched him stagger away clutching his stomach, and as soon as he left they keeled over, clutching theirs.

'Well,' said the senior steward shakily, 'It could o' been worser. I wanted to put nightshade in it.'

'I darn well wish you 'ad!' cried another, bolting for the rubbish tips.

Chapter 22

'R eady?' asked Tassie. She'd finally given in
to her urge to dress up in funny clothes,
and had put on a squire's tunic and
leggings that she'd found in the servants
quarters. The leggings were rather itchy, and she had
a feeling that there were a lot of other little life
forms in there with her, but all in all Tassie felt she
looked the part.

'Ready,' said Billy, blowing out his cheeks nervously.
Unfortunately for him, he had never been a boy who
could sulk or bear a grudge. While that made him a
lovely chap, it also meant that the anger he had felt
up in his room had been steadily leaking out of him.
Even though he was trying very hard, he was now
about as cross as a damp lettuce.

Tassie opened the door to the Great Courtyard and

Billy stepped out into the sunshine. The immediate effect was of someone turning the world's volume down sharply. The hubbub and bustling and bickering and laughing died instantly. Honoured guests and peasants seized up in mid-conversation. The fire-eater, who had just taken a huge mouthful of flame, went purple and nearly choked to death rather than break the silence by breathing out. His ears began to smoke. Everyone looked at Billy and tried hard to smile.

'Hello everyone!' Billy managed to hold up a hand and waggle his fingers in a wave. 'It's jolly nice of you all to come and support . . . er . . . well . . . the event, I suppose. King Pa will be ever so chuffed to see you, and do please help yourselves to as much food and drink as you want.' A thousand faces a-bulge with roast pig and pickled apples tried to avoid his eye.

'Oh, I see we have some people from Badspite here!' said Billy, spotting the crest on their tunics. 'Quite a lot of you. That's . . . er . . . nice. Well, welcome all! I would just like to say –' struggled Billy manfully. But at that moment, the door from Brutus's quarters thundered back on its hinges, and the Baron of Badspite himself filled the doorway – every square inch of it.

'Do I hear a chicken trying to squawk?' he shouted, hands on his hips and his monstrous legs astride. 'Miserable giblet! They've only come to see one person, and he's right over here, wearing my crest and holding this sword!'

The crowd turned to him as one, and a mighty roaring cheer spread through its ranks like water through a sponge. As Brutus strode out amongst them, they surged forward, swallowing him up in a human whirlpool. In seconds Billy and Tassie were left standing alone, looking at everyone's backs.

Billy watched the scrum at the other end of the courtyard for a moment.

'Are you sure they don't like him?' he asked Tassie.

'Positive,' said Tassie.

'Mm. I don't know . . .'

'Well, I do. Come on. You might as well find

your tent and get your armour on.' She dragged him off, looking out anxiously for Germlin Bilge, who had the next part in the Plan.

Two hundred yards away, Brutus was finding that the mean joy of making Billy feel small and unwanted waned fast. And he was wishing he'd put his armour on in his room, rather than have it sent down to the field. He'd had his back slapped so many times that his breakfast was trying to make a comeback. His neatly plaited hair was all messed up and had chunks missing where women had pulled it out for keepsakes, and he was black and blue from good-luck pinches, prods and pummellings. He hadn't realised that popularity was such a painful affair and if they didn't leave him alone soon, there wasn't going to be much left to take on Billy. It was unfortunate that being the people's hero suited his spiteful purposes right now, because he'd like to give each and every one of his well-wishers a very up-close-and-personal tour of the Huffington torture chamber. Which at the moment was housing Billy's watercolour collection.

'Gerroff!' he snarled, as one young man gave his upper arm a particularly nippy pinch.

'It's for luck!' smiled the man. 'And so's this!' He punched Brutus hard in the bicep, before melting back into the crowd. Brutus would have gone after him, but for three women still hanging on to his plait.

While Brutus and his swarm of 'supporters' crowded their way out of the main castle entrance, Tassie and Billy walked unnoticed out of a little side gate. They wobbled their way along a tree felled across the moat and began to troop down the track towards the field below. After a few minutes, Billy noticed that they were being followed. A small boy was marching along behind them, keeping a short distance away. Billy stopped.

'Hello, little boy!' he said. 'Oh! It's Germlin, isn't it? How's the plague coming along? The sores look better.'

Germlin stared up at him with the sort of brown eyes that would make a seal pup foam with envy.

'Much better thank you, Mithter Printhe,' he lisped is a small voice, as Tassie had taught him.

'Good. That's marvellous. I've always sworn by that minced vermin ointment,' said Billy, patting him on the head and then wiping his hand carefully on his short cloak.

'Mummy says that Sir Brutus'll sell me now I'm so much better,' said Germlin, sticking his thumb in his mouth and talking round it.

Billy winced.

'Tassie told us that you were going to save us, but Mummy said that you couldn't fight your way through fog. Is that true? Are we all going to be sold?'

Tassie picked up her cue. 'Of course he can fight!' she said hotly.

Billy opened his mouth.

'Billy wouldn't let anythin' happen to you kids and your families!' said Tassie with breezy confidence. 'He told me so himself, just an hour ago.'

'Er,' said Billy.

'And Billy promises that he will stop at nothin' to rid the Kingdom of Huffington of Sir Brutus. Don't you Billy . . .? Billy?'

'Er . . . yes,' said Billy.

Germlin sidled up and put his tiny, thin hand in Billy's.

'You're *very* brave. I think you're my hero.'

Tassie thought she might be sick if this went on any longer, but it was having the right effect on Billy, as she knew it would. For just a moment his noble lower lip wobbled, and then the steel started creeping back into his mild blue eyes. He straightened his back with a clank of armour.

'OK Germlin, mission accomplished,' she said out of the side of her mouth as she pulled Billy on his way down the hill. 'You were great! . . . I said you were great . . . Germlin, please go back to Mummy now . . .!'

But Germlin seemed not to hear. His hand was still locked in Billy's, the other thumb was still locked in his mouth and his enormous eyes never left the prince's face. It seemed that Billy was indeed a hero to somebody.

'Oh, for goodness' sake!' muttered Tassie with

exasperated affection, watching them lollop down the slope together. 'I just hope his sores aren't catchin'.'

There was much ceremony and fanfare down at the jousting field. The king mounted the Royal Pavilion and took his seat, waving regally as his soldiers encouraged the good folk of Huffington to cheer him loudly.

With Billy safely inside his stripy changing tent, left to the tender mercies of Lubbers and the unnerving gaze of Germlin Bilge, Tassie went off to check on the work of her partners-in-crime. Soldiers were already busy pushing the crowds back behind a rope barrier, leaving an arena long enough and wide enough for two men to batter each other off horses. Where the strip was cleared, the smell of freshly mown grass was almost overwhelming, and Tassie nodded her head approvingly before getting back down on all fours to make her way through the crush of people. This, she

211

quickly discovered, worked far better in modern times, when people hardly ever wore spurs or carried swords. Even so, in a short space of time, and with only minor wounds, she surfaced next to Brutus's tent, where Violetzka was waiting anxiously.

'Hello. Wow, you look amazing!' said Tassie, startled.

Violetzka was done up like a dog's dinner for the occasion. She had on a beautifully hand-stitched long blue dress, with the Royal Crest of Mazovia embroidered on the front, and the sort of sleeves that soak up your soup if you're not careful. Balanced on her head was an enormous cone shaped hat, with a veil feathering out of the top like a distress signal. In her arms she cradled a basket of red roses, and she was giggling madly to herself as she made a mock curtsey.

'About time you are 'ere!' she exclaimed in a whisper. 'Just in time for ze fun and ze frolicans. Ze big uckly bully 'as just gone into ze tent, and I sink zis is my cue.'

'Go girl!' Tassie hissed back. 'Good luck. Just don't lose your head and deck him.'

'I don't know vot zat is but it sounds like a goot idea,' sniffed Violetzka, then she picked up her skirts with an elegant hand and swept into the tent without knocking.

Tassie searched around frantically for a rip in the canvas. It took some moments before she got a beady eye glued to one, and then what she saw made her stuff her hand into her mouth to keep from laughing.

Brutus was standing in the middle of the tent. His mouth had dropped open and he kept staring round and rubbing his eyes. 'What in the name of Strange Sir Cecil of Stoke . . .?' he stammered. The whole tent was stacked from floor to roof with roses. The flowers that had once filled Violetzka's ample apartment were now crammed into this small space, piled on top of each other, and winding around the tent poles. He was about as chuffed as Violetzka to be on the receiving end of so much foliage. Rather less so in fact, because of the terrible 'itchy-scritchies and ze sneezy-wheezies'. He began to back away, his nose twitching, and bumped into Violetzka.

'Darlink! I knew you vood be pleased,' said Violetzka, waving a proud arm at the horticultural display. 'I sought to myself zis morning, vot can I do to show Bruty 'ow much I admire 'im?'

'You did?' Brutus was reeling from the rose fumes. He'd never considered Violetzka might actually *like* him!

'But of course! And I knew zese flowers would give you exactly the same pleasure as zey gave me,' she said with feeling.

Brutus looked around again like a trapped ferret. His eyes were already starting to itch, and Tassie could see a rash like bubble wrap popping up underneath his tunic.

'I don't know what to say, my lady,' he began cautiously, wriggling in his clothes, but Violetzka didn't let him finish. She bounded forward and pressed a gentle finger across his lips, taking care not to get punctured by the pointy beard.

'My love! Zere is no need for ze words!' she cried.

'Let ze stems speak for us. 'Ere,' she said, pulling out the roses one by one from the basket in her arms and placing them in his. 'A flower from your flower! See! I can be as vitty as you! You 'ave no idea 'ow long I have vonted to return ze compliment. You cannot know 'ow much I 'ave longed to reveal all my feelings for you!' It was a fabulous act. Tassie snorted with delight outside, and Brutus's eyes reddened in their scritchy sockets.

'Oh, Violetzka!' he managed, his throat tightening – mostly as part of the allergic reaction. 'That is indeed wonderful but . . .'

'Hush!' commanded Violetzka dramatically, tapping her finger sternly against his lips and nearly dislodging a tooth. 'It is right for ze knight to vear his lady's favour ven he faces ze Challenge, no?'

'No. I mean, yes,' said Brutus, trying to scratch his stomach without breaking the romantic mood.

'Goot,' said Violetzka, pulling out more rose petals from a drawstring bag inside her sleeve. 'Zese are my favours!' she announced. 'And it is ze custom in my country for ze knight to vear zem next to 'is skin. Under even ze vest.'

Tassie could see Brutus flinch from several feet away. His eyes now looked as if someone had drawn round them in red marker pen, tears streamed down his face, and marble-sized lumps were starting to appear all over his body.

'Next to the skin?' he asked faintly.

'Ya . . . so!' said Violetzka, and before he could stop her she'd pulled out the neck of his tunic and was emptying the bag vigorously down into the opening.

'Now you vill never forget vot I am zinking of you,' she said happily, shaking his tunic-front for good measure. 'Hokay. I am offski now. Ta ta.'

'But . . . but . . .' stammered Brutus, scratching himself furiously now. 'Can I not have one kiss before you go?'

Violetzka looked at him and laughed. 'Viz ze face like ze bag of pomegranates? I don't zink.' And she was gone in a flourish. Just in time too, because seconds later the tent was racked with a mighty 'WOOFOO!'

and something wet exploded across the canvas door. Tassie took her eye away, with the expression of one who has seen rather more than they wanted. 'WOOFOO!' came the noise again, and then again several times in rapid succession. The Plan seemed to be getting right up Brutus's nose.

Outside with Violetzka, Tassie was surprised to discover that the high five had been around long before Americans. The two clung together, crying with laughter, and every time the tent shook with another explosion, they laughed even harder. Finally Tassie had to steer them both away in case Brutus heard between sneezes.

'That was brilliant!' she said, mopping her eyes with Violetzka's veil. 'He won't be able to see Billy, let alone knock him off his horse!' She had a quick glance at the sun. 'Uh-oh, look at the time! You've got to get to your seat in the pavilion, and I need to make sure Billy is ready.'

'Tassie, you must do zis von zing for me,' said Violetzka, suddenly serious. 'You must give zis to

Billy, and tell him I vill never marry anyvon but 'im.' She fished out a fine, white silk handkerchief from one of her endless sleeves. ''E must pin it to 'is sleeve to show zat 'e is still my knight.' She handed it to Tassie and turned to go. Then she looked back.

'And tell 'im if 'e goes and gets killed, I vill personally knock ze block off 'im!' She nodded her pretty head sharply, and vanished into the crowd.

Chapter 24

Tassie ploughed her way back towards Billy's tent. The event was in full swing now, with reedy music blasting out from various flutes and whistles and bagpipe-type instruments. Tumblers were tumbling, acrobats were batting and guests with well-stuffed purses were simply falling over themselves to empty them at every stall and stand.

'Get your keepsakes here! Tournament keepsakes! Gems of the joust! Genuine bones! Original teeth! In a nice little velvet presentation bag! Get 'em while they rot!'

'Hold on a minute,' said Tassie to the stallholder, stopping for a look. 'Whose bones are these?'

'That over there wot you have your hand on, that is Prince William's femur, maiden. Genuine article, fresh off the body this morning! Only a groat, miss.'

'Billy's leg?' said Tassie, staring. 'But he's not even dead yet! How can you sell his bones?'

'Supply and demand, lady-luv,' said the man briskly. 'Today's relic buyer doesn't want to be hanging about waiting for decomposition you know. Here, how about this? The prince's right thumb on a chain. Look lovely round your pretty neck it would, maiden.' He held it up to the light.

'But . . . but . . . you don't even know he's goin' to lose!' said Tassie, bewildered.

The man tapped the side of his nose and winked.

'I don't have to, fair lady. Watch.' And he turned over the square of parchment advertising Billy's bones. It now said 'Genuine Wretched Bones of Poore Sir Brutus, two groats'.

'Two toes please,' said a young woman next to Tassie. 'And do you have any skull fragments of St Madge? You said you might be getting some in.'

She turned excitedly to Tassie. 'A couple more fragments and that's a set!' she said. 'It'll be my third one.'

'Your third St Madge?' said Tassie. 'That can't be right.'

'No, it is a bit greedy,' said the woman. 'My husband says I'll have to sell one. She's cluttering up the hall.'

'Well, I'd save your money on the prince bones,' said Tassie, giving the stallholder a dark look. 'Billy will be usin' them himself for a good few years to come.' And she stalked off with her nose in the air.

'So you could buy now and save yourself some money when his time comes!' shouted the man after her reasonably. 'Is that fair or is that fair? Tell you what, I'll throw in his horse's mane . . .'

The heralds were blasting away on their trumpets again as Tassie reached Billy's tent. There was a cheer from the crowd, and they suddenly surged towards the rope that surrounded the freshly made arena. Billy stuck his head out and looked around.

'Hello old thing!' he said, looking quite relieved on finding Tassie. 'Thought you'd seen sense and joined Brutus's merry band.'

'Yeah, right!' said Tassie, pushing him back inside

and following on. 'That loser! Are you sure that's your set of armour?' She looked him up and down. The armour seemed to hang off him sadly.

'I've tightened every strap and rivet,' said Lubbers accusingly. 'I believe Sire has been losing weight.'

'I didn't mean to,' said Billy, looking down. 'Funnily enough I've been a bit off my feed lately. Gosh, I've never seen armour that *sags* before!'

'That trumpet signal just now was the "Say your Prayers" alarm,' said Lubbers. 'Sire needs to be out in the field within two minutes.'

Tassie looked at Billy. He straightened up under her gaze and tried to look noble yet fierce – neither of which really came off. She took hold of his hand. (The other one was still occupied by Germlin.)

'You can do this you know,' she said, and, to her horror tears began to prick at her eyes. 'You are a hundred times the knight that Brutus is, and a thousand times a nicer bloke.'

'Now now, old girl. No need for blubbing,' said Billy, embarrassed. 'I'm quite happy. I'm going to go out there and give my cousin the thrashing he deserves. I'm going to do it for Germlin and the other Bilges; I'm going to do it for King Pa and his beloved honour. I'm going to do it so Brutus will never kick another puppy, or drown another servant. And I'm going to do it so Violetzka won't have to marry such a loathsome beast. As my poem goes:

"Be proud my pounding heart,
my knocking knees knock less.
Stand firm my armour!
(And my underpants and vest!) . . .""*

'Oh!' said Tassie quickly, sniffing. 'She gave me this for you!' She fished out the handkerchief and tied it tightly to one of Billy's arm-straps. 'She said she won't ever marry anyone else, but if you die she'll knock your block off.'

Billy looked down at the scrap of white lace on his arm and gulped. Gently he put down Tassie's hand, and Germlin's, and picked up his helmet.

'Madam,' he said, and bowed deeply. 'I shall never forget your kindness to me. Whatever happens today, I shall always remain your most loyal friend – as you have proved to be mine.' And he turned and left the tent.

Tassie blubbed loudly.

'Ahem. I think madam squire should fetch Sire's horse for him,' said Lubbers after a minute. 'He risks looking very foolish without it.'

'First in the arena – Prince William of Huffington, Heir to the Huffington Throne, Knight of the Royal Order of the Badger, Defender of Religious Things and Knower of Medical Magickery!'

Tassie followed Billy, leading Gramma towards the jousting arena. Gramma wore some fine armour of her own around her head and chest, and an extremely jaunty yellow silk horse-robe. Billy's coat-of-arms (a crossed quill pen and lute, and a rearing badger) was emblazoned down both sides.

Gramma kept trying to peer around at it as they

paraded before the cheering crowd. 'Would you look at the hand-stitching on this?' she said, oblivious to the occasion. 'Wonderful detail on the badger's eye! I'm more of a crochet person myself . . .'

'Stop!' cried Tassie, breaking into the flow of gibberish. 'Can we concentrate? The joust is about to start, and though I shouldn't say it myself, I think all the bits of the Plan are goin' really well!'

'Are they?' asked Gramma, still trying to sneak a look at her outfit from behind her armoured mask.

The trumpets sounded again, and all eyes swerved to where Sir Brutus would make his entrance. Necks were strained and hats removed for a good view. There was an enormous buzz of excitement in the air. Then Brutus appeared from his corner, leading Dastard himself as his latest squire had deserted that morning. The black horse danced and snarled and rolled its red eyes at the crowd, grinding the bit with his teeth. But Tassie's own eyes were on Sir Brutus of Badspite's armoured figure, as she waited gleefully for the next sneeze.

'Oh there you are, love!' Her mother was suddenly next to her, panting and dishevelled as she popped out from the crush of the mob. 'Has it started yet? I thought I was going to miss something . . . and I do so love a good scrap . . . s'cuse me, sir, would you mind turning your sword round the other way . . .? Thank you so much.'

'Hi, Mum.' Tassie didn't even turn round. She was still staring at Brutus. Her confident smile had frozen a little.

'Who's that?' asked her mother, leaning out across the rope rail. 'Oh! Brutus! Yoo-hoo! Sir Brutus!' she waved happily at the Black Baron. And then, to Tassie's horror, the Black Baron waved back.

'Mum,' she said, hardly daring to breathe. 'Have you been talkin' to Sir Brutus?'

'Only for a little while, dear. He was in such a bad way, poor chap, sneezing and coughing and scratching. The inside of his tent looked like the morning after a snail festival and he didn't think he was going to be able to joust! So I just gave him a hay fever tablet, that's all.'

At that moment, Brutus turned round and raised his visor to look Tassie full in the face with remarkably clear, un-reddened eyes. And he bared his terrible teeth in a wolfish smile.

Chapter 25

If Tassie had been the passing-out sort of girl, she would have hit the floor there and then. And if she hadn't loved her mother, who knows what might have happened with all those handy weapons about. As it was, there was nothing Tassie could do but twist the rope rail frantically in her hands and start praying as hard as she could for Billy.

The knights had already withdrawn to their separate ends of the field, and serfs were placing the wooden jousting rail down the length between them. Brutus, even in full armour and after his mammoth breakfast, swung himself easily up into Dastard's saddle. Billy, on the other hand, was inching himself up a mounting block as if scaling a mountain. His armour weighed quite a lot more than he did, and he didn't want to overbalance and end up as a pile of scrap.

There was a kerfuffle behind Tassie, and Violetzka and Bilge were spat out of the crowd beside her, followed by a few kicks and a good deal of cursing from the people they'd damaged on the way through.

'Vot is going on?' puffed Violetzka. 'Vere is ze sneezing? 'Alf ze guests are scratching zere eyes out, but ze fat bully? 'E is all better!'

'It be magic, that's what it be!' moaned Bilge, spitting on the ground and turning round three times to ward off evil. 'All that mowin' and scythin', by rights 'e should 'ave eyes the size o' goose eggs! It be magic or the devil, whar else can it be?'

'Um, have you two met my mum?' Tassie introduced them, then quickly stepped back between them to prevent any further chit-chat. Mrs Ripley was far more interested in the upcoming joust anyway.

'Ve must varn my Billy!' Violetzka said, craning her neck to watch her knight as he flopped over Gramma's back like a winded fish. 'Ve must tell him ze Plan 'as not vorked!'

'What's the point?' hissed Tassie. 'He didn't know

229

there *was* a plan! He can't be any more frightened than he already is up there, and at least he won't know that he's worse off than he was before. And anyway, some of the Plan *has* worked. Billy is going to stick up for himself and for everyone else. At least he has a chance . . .'

'Oh flummocks!' said Bilge, biting his fingers. 'Ol' king is startin' the joust!'

The king was rising to his feet. He waved one great hand, and the muttering stopped immediately. His heart swelled at the great sight of knights facing each other in Noble Conflict – it was just a shame that one of them happened to be his son.

'Honoured guests, friends, loyal hovel-folk!' he shouted. 'It both grieves me and fills with me with pride to witness the Challenge played out between my dear son, William, and my nephew, Sir Brutus of Badspite. The Challenge, once issued, must, by our Knightly Code, be answered! The loser, if he lives, will leave at once for the Crusades, never to return under pain of death. The winner receives the hand of the beautiful Lady Violetzka in marriage, and her enormous beetroot farm dowry. He will also inherit the entire Kingdom of Huffington – after I'm off the scene, of course.'

He looked left and right at the waiting knights. Brutus spat deliberately on to the ground.

'Gentlemen!' the king commanded. 'You may joust! May God have mercy on your souls!' He looked over to Brutus. 'Or whatever,' he finished lamely.

The heat was stifling as both horses reared and the crowd began to roar. The burnished shields and polished metal gleamed in the merciless sun. Brutus gave a great shout of rich, villainous laughter, spun Dastard in a tight full circle and unleashed him like a slingshot down the long grassy strip towards Billy.

Billy couldn't see him coming. He had propped open his visor with a twig because the eyeholes were way too high for him. Gramma's rearing up had snapped the twig and so Billy was flung forwards into mortal combat without being able to see what might be his last moments on earth . . .

But Brutus was not going to let his cousin off so lightly. Seeing Billy bouncing along, legs flapping and lance waving circles in the sky, Brutus thought he could have great fun toying with his victim for a while. After all, he had several hundred future loyal subjects to show off to.

As the horses thundered past each other, he held his lance out to the side and shouted 'Boo!' – landing a sideswipe across Billy's stomach that folded his armour like crumpled tin.

There was a muffled 'Oomph' from Billy, which reminded Tassie of their first meeting in the woods. She ducked under the rope and ran to Billy's end of the field as Gramma was trotting back. Out of the corner of her eye she could see Lubbers put Germlin into a headlock to stop him following her.

'What happened?' panted Gramma, peering out of her armoured mask.

'He's run me through, hasn't he?' coughed Billy weakly. 'I can't feel my legs!'

'No, he's only dented you,' said Tassie, examining

the deep groove across his belly. 'Jus' try to sit up straight.'

'I've jousted Brutus and survived? All my vital organs are still inside me! I have a poem for just such a moment . . .'

'No you haven't,' said Tassie grimly, feeling Gramma tense like a bucking bronco. 'Maybe later.'

'There might not be a later,' said Billy reasonably.

'Whatever,' said Tassie. She looked over at Brutus, already shouting abuse from the far end of the field, and pantomiming that he was dying of boredom. The Badspitians had begun some slow handclapping. 'Now are you holdin' on tight?' Tassie asked.

'Absolutely old thing,' quavered Billy, trying to look steely. 'Just point me at him! I'll show the brute what happens when one rumbles with a Huffington!'

'Would you like to take your lance too?'

'Oh yes. Good idea. Thank you sooooo –'

The rest of his sentence was lost as Gramma and Dastard galloped at each other like greyhounds with their tails on fire.

But it didn't get any better. Gramma did her best, trying to jink out of harm's way at the last moment, as the knights thundered past each other, but Brutus was literally having a field day. With every pass, he knocked more dents into Billy's armour, and Billy's body too, toying with him like a cat with a very confused mouse, and giving a triumphant 'Huzzah!' after every pass.

The Badspitians in the crowd loved it and cheered every blow, with bellowing gusts of laughter for good measure. The king sat and fumed. He'd always been ashamed of Billy's poor attempt at being a knight, but this lack of chivalry from the guests was intolerable.

'He's very good, that Brutus,' said Tassie's mum admiringly, as Billy finished a run with his helmet pushed round the wrong way. 'It's just a shame they couldn't find someone else who could make a good match of it. I'm pretty sure *I* could joust better than that other chap. He's rubbish!'

Tassie ground her teeth with fury, her hands over her eyes. She needed to do something, and do it fast. Billy could barely sit upright any more, and his brain must be liquid jelly after the battering his head had taken inside that tin can. Gramma's sleek white coat was foaming with the heat and the exertion. What, she wondered, could stop an evil, powerful brute like Brutus in full flow?

'Mum,' said Tassie slowly, 'where are the Twins?'

Chapter 26

There was a great roar from around the arena. Tassie turned just in time to see Brutus hit Billy at full gallop, and pound off down the length of the field with the hapless prince dangling limply on the end of his lance. Gramma didn't even seem to notice. She galloped straight on and out of the arena without him.

'Give us a blast on your horn. Quick!' Tassie told a nearby herald desperately, and as the ear-splitting notes deafened the crowd, she ran right up to where Sir Brutus had dumped Billy in a battered heap. He was just drawing his sword to jump down and finish the Challenge in the bloodiest way possible, when Tassie waved her hands for silence.

'HALF-TIME!' she shouted. 'WE'RE HAVIN' A BREAK COS SIR BRUTUS LOOKS A BIT

TIRED. GENTLEMEN, RETIRE TO YOUR TENTS. THERE WILL NOW BE A MUSICAL INTERRUPTION . . . ER . . . INTERLUDE . . . WHATEVER!'

Billy managed to rise on all fours and crawl around in dazed circles. Brutus tore off his helmet, glared at Tassie in disbelief and slammed his lance to the ground. He was about to take Tassie by the scruff of her tunic when Harry Bilge arrived, holding Germlin by the hand and surrounded by a grubby sea of excited peasant children.

'Ar-one,' said Harry to the other kids, exactly as Tassie had taught him. 'Ar-two, ar-one, two, three, four! Ta da-da-da-da-da-DAH, ta da-da-da-da-da-DAH, la la la LA, la la la LA!' And Huffs and Badspitians alike gaped in amazement as the children each grabbed the waist of the one in front, and set off in a robust conga around the arena. The Bilge kids, the kitchen wench and her pale-faced sisters, the young stewards who had somehow survived eating Brutus's cake, they all sang and kicked their legs as if their lives depended on it.

Brutus went a deep plum colour with rage, and yelled at the dancers to 'Stop, by all the demons!' But it was a catchy tune, and before very long the Head Cook had dropped her knives and had grabbed on to the back of the snake, while others rushed to join in. Bottoms large and small swayed around the grassy field. In all the kerfuffle, no one heard the deep rumble of thunder, or noticed the big, black clouds building. It was getting hotter.

The king stared at the scene of his loyal subjects high-kicking and trolling their way around the castle. He was absolutely furious.

'By all the Perky Pigeons of Prussia! What is all this about?' he roared at Tassie. 'Gadzooks, maiden, d'you think this is a Nine Men's Morris tournament? A Harvest Picnic? In case it has escaped your notice, this is a Challenge to the Death!'

'And in case it has escaped yours, it's your son that's about to be toast!' shot back Tassie, right up on her tiptoes and glaring into the astonished king's face above her. The king spluttered indignantly.

'Look, I can't stop the joust,' he protested. 'It's not allowed. Honour, honesty, valour and loyalty – it's what makes us knights!'

'Funny, I thought Billy had all that,' said Tassie, hands defiantly on hips. 'But you want him to die as well. It might make you some sort of knight, but it makes you a really lousy dad!'

Billy's father scowled at her and pointed at the jigging crowd. 'Well, I'm not having this nonsense. Stop it immediately! I am the KING!'

'Oh, get over yourself,' sniffed Tassie, and marched off to help Billy find his tent.

If the king was annoyed, Brutus was apoplectic as he stamped off towards his tent. That mad, infuriating tadpole of a girl had ruined his moment of glory! It would have taken him just five minutes to finish the miserable prince off for good and claim the kingdom. If Brutus had ever planned to let Billy off the hook, and send him to the Crusades instead of killing him – which he hadn't – then he forgot about that now.

But it would do the fools no good, thought Brutus with a snarl. The Rules of the Challenge said that when a knight was knocked from his horse, the Challenge would continue on foot. Brutus knew that Billy was even worse with a sword than a lance, if that were possible. Everyone would see the prince die and know who was master!

Unable to go into his tent because of all the roses, Brutus sat himself down on a grass bank under some trees and wiped his sweating forehead. He was so hot and damp inside his armour, he could feel his skin wrinkling, but he didn't care. His whole mind was focused on how he was going to kill Billy. Black clouds roiled, un-noticed, above him. And then suddenly, there was a child in front of him.

It was as though it had appeared from thin air, small and dirty, dressed in rags, with blond hair on end, and such a look of wicked mischief on its bright little face that Brutus blinked. He was just about to kick the brat away when it pointed a finger at him, threw back its head and laughed loudly.

'Poor, poor Sir Brutus!' said the child in a high, merry voice. 'He doesn't know!'

'Know what?' growled Brutus. He didn't like children at the best of times, and this certainly was not the best of times.

'He doesn't know what he doesn't know. Ner ner ne ner ner!' chirruped the child, and easily dodged the back of Brutus's hand as it came swinging round.

Poor old Brutus, cut and gored.
Killed by the magic in Billy's sword!'

'What are you talking about?' Brutus got up, getting angrier by the minute.

The child sang, skipping about just out of reach:

'Billy needn't fight too much,
because he has the magic touch.
Cut him, stab him, you can try,
but by his sword 'tis YOU shall die!'

★

'You're talking rot, you evil urchin,' snapped Brutus, and he bent down for a stone to sling at the child, who sped off, laughing into the crowd.

'Revolting little jackanapes . . .' he muttered, turning away. 'AAARGH!' He nearly leapt out of his armour as he found the jackanapes was now somehow standing right behind him. 'Odsplut! What sorcery is this?' he roared, the sweat pouring out of him. The child giggled and chanted:

'Billy has a Magic Sword,
and he's not scared of you.
Think you'll kill him? Not a hope.
He'll split you right in two!'

'Complete tosh!' Brutus felt a stab of superstitious fear, and fought it hard. There was no such thing as sorcery, he told himself. This mangy mudlark was just pulling his chain – and he reached forward to grab the brat by the hair so he could teach it some Badspitian manners.

Just as he did so, there was a huge crash, and a bolt of brilliant light ripped the sky apart. Brutus leapt in the air, his heart pounding. And the child vanished once more! The Black Baron was now seriously frightened. He cringed away and made the sign of the cross – something he hadn't done since he was kicked out of the Church for cheating.

'Ha ha!' giggled the voice, just above his head. Brutus screamed and looked up. The brat was lying along the branch of a tree above him and wagging a playful finger. The Black Baron moaned. He knew now this thing was not human, for nothing could move that quickly. He was being taunted by a demon!

'Leave me alone!' he cried, backing away. There was another crash of thunder, and when the lightning came it made the child's eyes glow like flames. Brutus turned and began to run. He only got a couple of steps when yet *again* the raggy urchin appeared, hopping up and down demonically right in front of him, and making terrible faces at him! He fell to his knees.

'Don't hurt me. Please don't hurt me!' he sobbed.

'Don't see why I should,' hissed the child mockingly, 'when Prince Billy's Magic Sword is going to kill you dead as dead in ten minutes!' The urchin shook its spiky blond head pityingly, and dragged a grubby finger very slowly and agonisingly across its throat. Brutus's jaw dropped slack with terror. He moaned again and, hiding his face in the dirt, tried to crawl away. Sam looked up at Lil in the tree, and they both stuffed their hands in their mouths to stop the laughter.

Chapter 27

You puts yer left leg in . . . yer left leg out! In, out, in, out and you shakes it all about . . .'

While Brutus was being tormented, most of the Huffs were now on the Tournament field, led by some very excitable children. They were all enjoying this new sport enormously.

'. . . you does the 'Okey Cokey and you turns around . . .'

The visiting Badspitians looked on, scowling scornfully. *They* didn't dance. It was, in fact, against the law in Badspite, along with 'merrymaking', and any song that didn't include the line 'Sir Brutus is the Greatest Man Who Walked on Two Legs'.

'. . . and that's what it be about – Oy!'

The dancers didn't even notice the big spludges of rain that were just starting to fall. It was altogether too much to remember which leg was going in, what was being shaken about, and which way to turn to avoid breaking your nose on a neighbour's breastplate.

The Twins came bowling across the grass to where Tassie waited with Billy and a herald.

'We got him! We got him!' they squawked, bouncing up and down with glee. 'Done like a kipper! That Big Bum of Badspite . . .!'

Tassie high-fived them both and gave them a big hug. 'Well done, guys . . .'

'Can we go and frighten someone else?' asked Lil, looking around eagerly for another victim. 'We're REALLY brilliant at it!'

'Not jus' yet,' said Tassie. 'Its time to restart the Challenge. Will you two go and hide for a while? I don't want Brutus to see that we tricked him.'

'OK,' said Sam. 'C'mon Lil, lets go blow spit-balls at the king!'

Tassie knew of no one that deserved spit-balls blown at them more than the King of Huffington.

'Off you go then. Have fun,' she said, then turned and dug the herald in the ribs. 'Give 'em all a tootle, Mr Herald. It's show time!'

It was the heavy rain that actually stopped the dancing, and even then Tassie could still hear, 'WHOA-O the 'Okey Cokey! Knees bent, arms stretched, rah rah rah,' from various corners of the field. The sky had gone very dark, and most people crammed themselves under stalls and into tents, wriggling for a good view. Tassie was wondering where Gramma had got to. There had been no sign of her since she galloped out of the arena, but then an awful hush fell on the crowd, and all other thoughts fled as Sir Brutus of Badspite walked slowly into the field. Lightning crackled under the low, boiling clouds, and peasants whispered that the Black Baron had never looked more menacing as he stopped and waited for his opponent. Suddenly they remembered that they were just about to see the grisly death of the very nicest prince that Huffington had ever had.

In fact, Brutus had never felt less mean in his life. It had taken every scraping of whatever courage he had not to turn tail and run when he heard the herald's fanfare. The only thing that kept him going was that he was even more terrified of being sent to the Crusades than he was of Billy's Magic Sword.

'Evil urchin! It's all lies and wickedry!' he told himself, but he jumped at every crack of thunder, and his hands trembled inside their gauntlets.

'. . . And I'm not wearing this!' said Billy, fighting his way out of the silver helmet and throwing it over his shoulder. 'I can't see a thing out of it, and the rain noise is making my ears ring. If Brutus *is* going to kill me, I at least want to know it's happened!'

'Well, OK,' said Tassie doubtfully. 'Hopefully you won't need it anyway. Here, I'm your squire, let me carry your sword.'

This time Tassie led the prince out. The rain soaked her leather slippers in moments, but she didn't notice. She was busy counting the seconds between each fork of lightning. She was going to put the cherry icing on the Twins' cake.

'. . . Nine, TEN,' she counted under her breath, and thrust the sword towards the sky as it lit up with a great jag of lightning, bang on time. Thunder roared like a cannon and the sword flashed and gleamed, like something Magic and Holy in the midst of the storm. Sir Brutus jumped a full two feet back. Billy took the sword in both hands and faced him. The king gave the signal . . . and Brutus lost his nerve and ran.

It couldn't really be called 'running away' mused Tassie, because Sir Brutus was too big and too muscle-bound to do more than shamble quickly. The Huffs roared with surprised approval, as Prince Billy, after scratching his head in bafflement, broke into a metallic, jogging gait after the Baron. The Twins peeked out from behind a tent flap and screeched with laughter, shouting at Billy, 'Wave your Magic Sword! Slice him in two! Yeeeee Hoooo!'

'Well, I *suppose* that's better,' said Tassie's mum

doubtfully. 'But it would look more realistic if they did actually fight a bit.'

'It's complete tosh, that's what it is,' snorted Mr Ripley beside her. 'Someone ought to show them how it's done!' He ducked under the rope, and to Tassie's horror, she saw him stride through the driving rain towards the lolloping, breathless knights.

'Daddy!' shrieked Sam and Lil desperately, running to the side of the arena. 'Come back Daddy! Pleeease! Oh, you're *spoiling* it. You don't get it . . .'

'I certainly do get it,' said Mr Ripley, without breaking stride. 'Here, you two knight chappies! You haven't got a clue, have you?'

Billy and Brutus both halted, puffing, in surprise.

'Now watch me . . . come on – closer, so that you can see. Do hurry up! Here we go, *thrust* . . . and parry, and *stab*, and riposte . . . see what I'm doing?' Mr Ripley demonstrated, while Billy and Brutus gawped at him. 'If you don't do it properly someone is going to get hurt, and it could be our Tassie. She's my Precious Possum and I won't allow it.'

'Oh, DAD!' Tassie howled, agonised. She didn't know which was worse, being called a Precious Possum in front of all these people, or seeing yet another plan in peril.

'Oh Dad nothing, young lady,' scoffed her father. 'If you and the Twins over there must get involved in these sorts of shenanigans, then I have to look after you.'

'Twins?' The ice-chip eyes behind Brutus's visor lit up, and he turned to look where Mr Ripley pointed. Too late, Sam and Lil yelped and hid behind a stall.

Mr Ripley didn't even notice.

'Now please can we see a *proper* fight, gentlemen? Come on, Tassie.' And her dad stalked off in the direction of the mead tent without a backward glance.

'TWINS!' roared Brutus, rounding on Tassie and Billy, his sword slashing through the air. Raindrops flew from his armour, and thunder cracked overhead.

'Run, Billy!' shouted Tassie 'Run away. Please!'

'I'm afraid I cannot do that, old girl . . .' said Billy gravely, gripping his own sword tighter. Tassie suddenly thought how noble he looked.

'. . . I think my boots have rusted up. It'll be a fight to the death now, I fear. Do stand back, old thing.'

But Brutus wasn't even looking at Billy. All his anger was bubbling and burping to the surface as he finally realised that everything that had gone wrong for him was Tassie's doing: the twenty-course breakfast that sat in his stomach like a clutch of cannonballs; the violent friendliness of the Huffs; the freshly-mown grass and the ludicrous dancing; and most especially those evil, evil Twins! It was ALL . . . HER . . . FAULT!

'Death to the Half-Frog!' he screamed, his voice almost lost amongst the yelling of the crowd, and he raised his sword high as he hurtled towards her.

Then, it seemed to Tassie, everything happened in slow motion. She turned and tried to run for the crowd. She could almost feel the blade between her shoulders, and her legs just wouldn't move fast enough . . . Tassie was twenty feet from safety when she heard a triumphant shout of evil laughter right behind her and the clanging of armour. Everyone behind the rope was yelling and pointing over her shoulder, urging her to run faster.

Billy couldn't work out what was happening. The rain lashed his face, and it took every ounce of strength just to put one foot in front of the other. He saw Brutus tower over Tassie, and stopped to dash water from his eyes for a better look. Horror spread across his face . . .

'Tassie, beware!' he cried, as the thunder rolled and crashed again.

'Die Tadpole!' howled Brutus, whirling his sword around his head as he towered above her. The king jumped up, speechless with horror at the knight who was about to kill a child. Tassie saw the giant figure blot out the sky; heard the crack and crick of twisting armour and the whistle of the whirling blade . . . she shut her eyes and turned her back to fend off the fatal blow . . .

Billy hit her like a runaway train, knocking her sideways with all the breath thumped out of her body. She rolled over and opened her eyes just in time to see Brutus's look of surprise as his sword hissed down through empty air. So much weight had he put into that final blow that it took just one furious swipe from Billy's sword to knock him into the air and then flat on his face with a teeth-rattling crunch.

'You were going to kill Tassie!' shouted Billy, hopping around his cousin like a demented crow. 'That's . . . that's . . . that's really not the done thing around here, you OAF!' And he kicked Brutus extremely hard on the bottom. Brutus yelped and got up on all fours, groping blindly for his sword.

'Kick him again!' urged Tassie with what was left of her breath, and to her surprise, Billy did.

'And this is for pushing me out my bedroom!' he said. Whump!

'And this is for trying to steal my lady-love!' he said. Whump!

'And this is for selling off the children!' he said. Whump!

Each 'Whump!' laid Brutus out afresh. Billy picked up the Black Baron's sword and threw it out of harm's way.

'*I* am the Prince of Huffington,' Billy said. 'So there!'

Brutus lay still, completely winded and wondering how long it was going to be before his breakfast got the better of him. At last he gave in, and threw up the Pig's Trotter Pie.

Chapter 28

The crowd cheered and yelled and thumped each other on the back in delight.

This was a turn-up for the books all right! The relic-seller made sure no one was looking and turned his sign over. Pickpockets pulled their hands out of people's pockets long enough to clap. Brutus rolled over into a puddle and stared at Billy with utter amazement, like a circus prizefighter that had been hit out of the ring by a ballet dancer. Billy just looked stunned. Brutus started to growl . . .

'Lubbers!' croaked Tassie from the ground, pointing muddily over his shoulder, and everyone in the field spun round to look.

Billy's manservant stood motionless on a hill, his superior nose silhouetted against the sky. Then he beckoned with one delicate finger . . . and over the rise came the remaining Bilge children, running barefoot. And behind them, other kids: big, small, all of them thin, first in their tens, then in their hundreds, and then, like ants on the ground as they ran towards the arena, in their thousands. The wave of urchins and jackanapes hit the crowds at full tilt, screaming like banshees. They climbed over adults, they scrambled through trees, they ran over stalls. They shook their skinny, dirty mitts in the air and yelled at the top of their voices, 'BRAVO FOR BILLY! BASHINGS FOR BRUTUS!'

'Uh-oh,' grinned Tassie to Brutus, 'I wouldn't want to be in *your* tin shoes!'

Brutus's bewildered eyes grew wider and wider as the tidal wave of humanity swept towards him. Tassie saw Violetzka and Harry Bilge take up the howl as they joined the racing children. There was the boy with the bear, all the stewards and pageboys and squires that Brutus had beaten since he arrived, and behind them, masses of urchins, wretches and brats, ripping off the 'For Sale' notices around their necks.

So close was the heaving, seething mass of mostly unwashed, hysterical children, that Brutus could see the whites of their eyes and the green of their teeth, as well as a fairly good view of their tonsils. He started to back away, panicking, searching for a way out, or a stone to crawl under. He slipped in his haste and as he dropped on all fours, the crowd broke over him. All he could see was the blur of legs – skinny and sunburnt, white and wobbly, straight and knock-kneed, legs with dog-bites, legs with flea-bites, legs with open running sores . . . Brutus curled up into as much of a ball as he could manage in full armour, and screamed like a frightened baby while he waited for them to take their revenge . . .

But in the end, none of the children took the blindest bit of notice of him. None of them even bothered to slow down as they stampeded over him. They were heading for a very startled Billy, who, until three seconds ago, had his eyes shut and was halfway through the Knight's Miraculous Victory Prayer for the third time. In moments he was hauled, dazed and confused, up on his feet, and from there, on to Harry Bilge's sturdy shoulders.

Lubbers appeared smoothly at Tassie's shoulder.

'I believe these are the urchins the mistress required?'

'Lubbers, you're amazin'!' cried Tassie. 'You're not goin' to believe this, but Billy really did beat Brutus – on his own and everythin'!' She remembered Brutus's growl as he lay on the ground. 'But it's a good job you came when you did! "A stitch in time" my mum always says.'

'Does she indeed?' said Lubbers politely. 'Well, if the mistress would excuse me, one seems to have acquired a great many lice . . .'

'They really do love him, don't they?' said Tassie, gazing around at the scene of joyful chaos.

'Oh yes, madam. I believe it is all that vermin paste.'

Billy was almost invisible inside an excited, happy scrum as Tassie fought her way towards him.

'You did it!' she shouted over the racket, her eyes

shining. 'You beat the Bully of Bad Smell!'

'Th-that c-can't be r-right,' said Billy bouncing up and down and confused. 'He must have been just resting before he diced me like a turnip!'

'You flattened him!' screamed Tassie, laughing. 'You saved this damsel in distress, and you're definitely the people's favourite. That's a winner – not who can cut the biggest chunks off who!' And all of a sudden she was on Harry Bilge's shoulders, punching the air and pulling Billy's arm up in a victory wave. The crowd went wild.

'Do you know,' said Billy, smiling suddenly, 'I believe I can feel a poem coming on!'

'Flippin' heck. Well, if you have to . . .'

'Oh bad, the blackest knight, and rotten thru! –
He cheated, lied! – his manner thuggish!
Then we all kicked his bottom. S'true!
Huffs are heroes. Brutus is rubbish!'

Tassie was still pogoing away in the crowd five minutes later, when, for the second time that day, someone knocked every last ounce of breath from her and the world went dark.

'Ow . . . Mum!' she managed, trying to free her arms from the bear hug. 'Could you mind my ribs – they're a bit bruised.'

Her mother laughed and hugged her again. 'You can stop acting now!' she crowed. 'Gosh, you were good. And I was absolutely *convinced* Sir Brutus was going to skewer you like a kebab! It gave me a few anxious moments I can tell you . . .!'

'Vere is 'e? Zat big low-life!' Violetzka stumbled up to the party, flushed with excitement. Her hat was all askew, and she'd rolled up her lacy sleeves to drag behind her the biggest, spikiest mace that she could lay her hands on. 'Now it is my turn to bash ze bully! Vere is ze vorm?'

She suddenly caught sight of Billy, gave a loud screech in Mazovian and dropped the mace to fling her arms round him – which put both him and Harry Bilge flat on their backs on the grass.

Things were developing over in the crowd too. The Badspitians had travelled to the joust hoping to steal land and make the Huffs slaves. Now that Brutus had lost the day, they were giving their disappointment a very free rein. Drawing swords, they fell upon the Huffs even before they could put down their pigeon drumsticks. Within seconds, the biggest, noisiest fight that Tassie had ever seen was carrying on all round her. The king ordered everyone to be quiet or else, and then stalked off in a paddy when they ignored him. The Huffs were taken by surprise, but it was in their nature to scratch and gouge first and ask questions later. It wasn't long before the Badspitians were getting the worst of it. Even the Bearded Lady had one unfortunate visitor in a headlock while Tassie's dad attacked him with the sharp end of a very angry rooster. Everywhere was chaos.

'Billy!' shouted Tassie, still a little muffled by her mum's hug. 'Billy! Violetzka – put him down for two minutes, will you? Billy, we have to find Brutus. We must show he's defeated or you'll have baddies queuin' from here to next Christmas wantin' to try their luck!'

'I'll find ze miserable dog!' screeched Violetzka, snatching up her spiky weapon again and glaring round murderously.

For a moment Billy seemed to savour the lovely thought of unleashing the wrath of Violetzka on the fleeing Brutus . . . but then he braced himself and reached for his enemy's sword.

'Sorry, Violetzka old thing, I love you very much, and I was lost in admiration when you wrestled that wolf on Witchburning Wednesday, but I rather think this is my shout. After all, it would be such a waste if you ended up winning your own hand in marriage.'

'You 'ave already won, you seelly man!' scoffed

Violetzka. 'Let somevon else 'ave a bit of fun!'

At last, after no end of a scene – in which Tassie announced she was going with Billy, Mrs Ripley expressly forbade it and said they were going home and Tassie said she'd like to see her try going home; and in which Violetzka said that if Tassie was going with Billy, she certainly was, and Mrs Ripley said no, Tassie wasn't, she was going home with the family and that was that – the whole group trotted off to track down Brutus. It wasn't tricky. All they had to do was follow the trail of groaning, injured peasantry that had been in his way as he fled.

'He can't have gone too far,' said Tassie, helping a blacksmith pull his head free from a rabbit hole. 'Not with all that armour on.'

In fact Brutus hadn't got very far. He'd headed for the woods, believing he might lose any pursuit in the trees. But he'd only gone a few strides into the dripping foliage, when he heard a voice just above his head.

'He's Brutus of Badspite,
and folks say he's silly,
he's rubbish at fighting –
can't even beat Billy!'

'I was going to beat him!' roared Brutus, screeching to a halt and scanning the branches above his head. 'The fight wasn't over!'

''Tis now,' said the voice. 'Look. I'm over here! Are you *really* so useless you can't see me?'

'No,' Brutus said with dangerous calm, having caught sight of Sam lolling on his branch. 'And I'm not so useless that I can't tear a revolting, tricksy little midden-hound like you into twenty bloody pieces. And your twin too, wherever he's hiding! Yaah!' He lunged up to grab Sam's dangling, bare foot and yank him to the ground.

'Actually, I'm a she!' said Lil, tucking herself into a little ball right behind Brutus's knees.

Brutus half turned to look for her, and in that split second Sam launched himself at Brutus's head, knocking the Black Baron flying. He tried to stagger back, went straight over Lil, somersaulted into a small dell, and ended face down in the brambles at the bottom. By the time Tassie and the others came puffing round the corner, Lil was perched regally on his backplate, and Sam was shoving handfuls of a red ants' nest down his armoured trousers.

'He's our prisoner!' chirped Lil happily to Tassie. 'If you want him, you have to ask nicely.'

'Please, please get me away from these urchins,' asked Brutus nicely, wriggling with ants.

'Not you,' said Sam, and bashed his helmet with a stick.

'Please Twins, you've done an amazin' job, and can we now take your prisoner back to the field?' asked Tassie, only too happy to do it nicely, because they deserved it.

Her mother had rather different ideas. 'You two – get off that poor man!' she ordered shrilly. 'I'm so sorry, Mr Brutus. They really are a handful. I think it might be the orange squash.' And she hauled the Twins up by an arm each giving them each a little shake.

'Say sorry to Mr Brutus, Sam, Lil.' But luckily she had dragged them, kicking and whining, back up the path towards the castle before either Twin could refuse to do any such thing. 'Look at the state of you! I just hope the police have gone, and we can tidy you up a bit in the loos.' Her voice faded into the foliage.

Once up on his feet, Brutus started to regain a little bit of his attitude as well as a more human colour.

'So. You think you can take me back, *Prince* Billy?' he sneered, getting to his feet and rippling his muscles under a coating of leaf mould and armour.

'No,' said Billy seriously. 'But I think a few thousand Huffs might have a good stab at it!'

Chapter 30

The storm had passed over and the sun was peeking through the clouds again. Back at the field, the crowd fight was still in full flow. Mounting the steps of the Pavilion, Tassie spotted Gramma on the field just below the rail. She was busily laying out two Badspite pikemen with one sweep of her hind hoof.

'Gramma! I wondered where you'd got to! Are you all right?' Tassie asked, leaning over the rail to talk to her.

'Yes, dear. Just had a few things to sort out with MoOD.' Gramma waited until another Badspite soldier came running past, and her hoof flashed out again. 'Gosh, it's fun this, isn't it?'

'Well, jus' hurry up and fill your boots,' said Tassie. 'Billy's about to stop the party.'

Billy picked up the herald's horn and shouted to Tassie over the hubbub, 'I don't suppose you could make this work? I could never find the strings on these things.'

'I'll do my best,' said Tassie, shaking the herald's spit out of the instrument unhappily. 'It won't be anythin' to dance to, but I might get a squeak out of it!'

It turned out to be a series of drawn-out farting noises, but it did the job. After a while people stopped fighting and looked around to see where that dreadful racket was coming from. Billy cleared his throat.

'Now everyone just jolly well listen,' he began. He wasn't shouting, but his voice carried clearly across the field. 'There are far too many fights going on when there was only one on the bill for today, and Brutus and I have finished. If you'd like to carry on killing each other, please organise your own event. Arthur Bilge, I saw what you did with your elbow earlier, and if you ever want to be a squire of mine you'll say sorry.'

Arthur blushed and beamed at the same time, and offered a sporting hand to the Badspitian he was kneeling on, who promptly bit it.

Billy looked around the Pavilion.

'Well,' he said uncertainly, 'it seems that King Pa has decided to take an early lunch break, so if you'll all forgive me, I'm going to fill in with a spot of kinging while he's gone. Bring in Sir Brutus!'

Tassie blew another raspberry on the horn as Sir Brutus was led, unarmed and with his hands bound, to stand in front of the Pavilion, his great black head hanging in defeat. He was under close guard from the Head Cook, who kept prodding him in the ribs with a spit-roast skewer and uttering dire threats which, fortunately for him, he couldn't understand.

'Sir Brutus of Badspite. Do you admit yourself defeated?' boomed Billy, in a fine imitation of his father.

'Yes,' muttered Brutus.

'Sorry? Didn't catch that,' boomed Billy again, cupping his ear theatrically.

'Yes! I'm defeated, all right? Get on with it,' shouted Brutus.

The crowd began huzzah-ing, but Billy flapped at them to shut up.

'And are you sorry for all the fuss you've caused?' he asked Brutus.

'What? Oh. Yes, I suppose so.'

'And you won't ever do it again?'

'Well, it's pretty unlikely, isn't it?' snapped Brutus.

Pause.

'And was that a yes or a no?' intoned Billy.

The Head Cook skewered Brutus threateningly.

'It was a no. No, I won't do it again! Happy?'

Pause.

'And who is the boldest, bravest and cleverest knight in the whole wide world?'

'Oh, get on with it,' hissed Tassie. 'I know you're totally amazed to still be alive, but that's no excuse. You're s'posed to be decidin' on Brutus's fate.'

'I'd like to kill him!' whispered back Billy fiercely. 'He's been terribly mean to everyone!'

'You what?' Tassie was shocked. It had never occurred to her that Billy might extract his own bloody revenge.

'No, wait a minute. I'd like to *want* to kill him, that was it. He really does deserve a jolly good executing with a rusty sword.'

'Yes, but you can't . . .'

'Do you think he could be reformed?' Billy mused, staring at Brutus thoughtfully. 'I mean, he could be quite useful – you know, for invasions and national sporting events and catching rats and stuff, if he could only keep his hands off other people's kingdoms. Perhaps if I read him poetry . . .'

'. . . I think he'd beg you for execution,' interrupted Tassie.

Billy looked hurt. He turned back to the expectant crowd.

'Fellow Huffingtonians!' he cried, raising his hands. This time there was an enormous cheer, accompanied by whistling and stamping. The cannier Badspitians finally called it a day and tore the Black Baron's coat-of-arms from their tunics.

'Huffingtonians!' cried Billy again. 'We need to decide on the fate of my kinsman, the bad Sir Brutus of Badspite. Who's got a coin?'

After a moment a Huff penny landed on the platform.

'And I want it back!' shouted the thrower.

Billy looked at the marks on one side of the coin.

'Right, "King Pa" – we pack him off to the Crusades, never to darken our leafy lanes again, lest we change our minds and lop his bonce off. And . . .' he turned the coin over, ' "Badger Rampant" – we find him something useful to do here . . .'

The coin flew up and up into the air and Brutus covered his eyes.

Chapter 31

'ell, that's it,' said Tassie to Gramma as she came trotting across the grass. 'It's all over. Billy's learnin' to be hero-worshipped, and Violetzka is writin' weddin' invitations.'

'Jolly well done! I knew you could manage it! Soon as I saw you I said to myself, that girl's got a bit of pluck and gumption . . .'

'Yuck,' said Tassie, who didn't like the sound of pluck *or* gumption. 'Well, you missed all the good bits.'

They began to follow the back of the parade up to the castle entrance, picking their way through the remains of an eventful day – litter, half-eaten food, drinking horns and roving corpse-robbers.

'What did MoOD say?' asked Tassie, as one such robber reached for her pocket. 'EXCUSE ME!

That's mine and I'm not dead yet!' The corpse-robber slithered away disappointedly.

'They weren't very happy,' said Gramma cheerfully. 'I've been a bad horse, letting your family into the Past.'

'Oh dear,' said Tassie.

'But you saved Billy, so there wasn't much they could do really. I got a warning.'

'Which means what?'

'Which means I put it with the others,' said Gramma. 'They don't scare me. Well, not much. Well, yes they do actually. Anyway, you go off and join the fun. I need a snack.'

Tassie ran over the drawbridge and through the portcullis of the main entrance. The courtyard was a riot of dancing and merrymaking, especially now everyone was reasonably sure that Good had triumphed, and Bad was out on its ear. Billy and Violetzka were up on two empty barrels of mead – the only sort they had left – while the people jigged and sang all round them. Germlin had somehow escaped from the long arm of Lubbers again, and was firmly clamped around Billy's right leg.

'Oh Tassie!' shouted Billy, waving like a windmill. 'Come over here! I've been looking for you.'

Tassie forced her way through the mob, and Bilge upended a barrel for her. Billy grabbed her hand shyly and pumped it up and down.

'I don't know what to say, old thing. You made us all stand up for what we believe in and we're jolly, jolly chuffed and thankful and everything,' he stammered emotionally.

'Plan A was a bit of a wash out, I'm afraid. It was a really good plan,' Tassie said modestly, because she knew that it was, 'but I hadn't told my mum. The Hokey Kokey was the Bee's Bananas though!'

'Well, it all taught me a thing or two!' cried Billy, wobbling on his barrel. 'I'd be in little pieces in a package addressed to "No 1, The Crusades" if it hadn't been for you. It's thanks to you we have a kingdom. Thanks to you the children are safe, and thanks to you I'm going to be married to my beautiful Violetzka an hour from now . . .'

'Forty-seven minutes, on ze dottle,' said Violetzka.

'We'd be awfully pleased if you'd be bridesmaid,' said Billy.

'Really? Cool! I mean, I'd be honoured . . . I'll have to get changed though . . .'

'. . . and best man too, if you wouldn't mind.'

'Er, no. Not if you're short.'

'It's just that we don't want anything else to go wrong, and you seem to have a knack with the unexpected.'

And a good thing too, thought Tassie to herself. After all the commotion the Balloon was straining to push her back to her own time again. It felt like vacuuming your stomach on full power, and it was getting stronger. Tassie knew that she'd have to leave very soon.

'Long live King William!' shouted a peasant (it sounded a lot like Bilge), and the cry was taken up around the courtyard.

'Shush! Shhhhh!' flapped Billy. 'It's jolly nice of you and all that, but poor old King Pa will blow an artery if he hears you going on in that treasonous sort of way. He might bring back Death by Tripe and Greased Rat!'

The crowd went very quiet and pale and made throwing-up expressions at each other. The torture had only ever been used once. That had been an accident due to a misunderstanding between the king, the Head Cook and a very unfortunate dinner guest. Now the threat alone was enough to quell rebellions.

Into the silence strode Lubbers the manservant. Lesser mortals might have run pell-mell, panting for breath and bouncing off bystanders in order to gasp out the vital news before their lord. Lubbers managed the same sense of urgency by walking slightly faster than usual, and coughing loudly behind people who stood in his way.

'Gadzooks man, what is it?' cried Billy, alarmed.

'Sire,' said Lubbers calmly. 'I believe the king is on his way and would like a word.' And indeed behind him came the giant King Pa, stomping through peasants, lords and ladies in all his finery, his eye fixed sternly on Billy.

'Oh dear,' said Billy.

'That,' growled King Pa, 'is exactly what I thought. I've never been so ashamed in all my life. After all the lessons I gave you, and the example I set you! I can't believe what happened today!'

Billy hung his head. 'It was a very poor show, I'm afraid. I never really got the hang of armour, and hurting things makes my nose bleed . . .'

'I haven't finished yet!' the king snapped. He crossed his great arms and glowered at Billy. 'I'm ashamed of *myself* because you showed me what a fool I've been. You might not be the son I always wanted, but today you are a son of whom I'm very proud. You stood up for our people and, without doubt, you are a very brave and honourable knight.' And to everyone's total amazement, the king took the crown off his own head, and placed it on Billy's.

'You really do deserve this,' he said grudgingly. ' It always made my head ache anyway. It's no fun being a king, but I suppose it must help if people like you.' He glared pointedly round at the crowd, and strode off back into the castle.

Everyone blew out their cheeks with astonishment. Billy tried to lift the crown from where it had slipped down over his nose.

'Long live King William?' tried Bilge again, sure he must be on to a winner this time, and indeed a great cheering arose and the dancing started up again.

Tassie gazed around at the laughing, smiling faces and felt a stab of pride. She certainly hadn't been alone in saving Billy and the kingdom, but there was no doubt at all who the brains of the outfit had been.

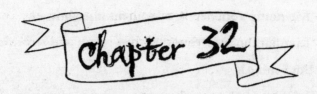

Chapter 32

'And do you, Violetzka Agnieszka Beatrycze Kaczmarek, take William Arthur Ricbert Huffington to be your lawful wedded husband . . .'

'Ricbert!' snorted the watching children, giggling. The sun was once more hot above the Rose Arbour, and the entire audience for the joust had now become welcome wedding guests, standing and sitting on the grassy banks beneath the castle.

'It's a thuper name,' said Germlin, with his thumb still wedged in the corner of his mouth.

'My name's Ricbert,' said one of the others shyly.

'Really? We thought it was Rupert!'

'Yes, well, I thought Ricbert sounded silly. I didn't realise it was *royal*!'

There was a pause.

'My name's Ricbert too,' said another boy.

'Liar liar, hose on fire!'

'And mine.'

'Juliette, you're a *girl*!'

'I meant Ricberta.'

'Shhh!' hissed Tassie from behind the happy couple where she was coping with armfuls of Violetzka's wedding train, and juggling the two rings, terrified of losing the Huffington family heirlooms.

It was during the romantic clinch at the end of the service that Tassie saw her mother madly waving at her from the back of the crowd. 'Home,' she was mouthing crossly. 'Right now!' Tassie couldn't see below her shoulders, but she knew from experience that she had each twin in a vice-like grip, and would only release them when the car door was open and all the exits blocked. Tassie felt the tug on her own intestines and knew she really did have to leave.

She tapped Billy on the arm. She had to do it a couple of times actually, but eventually he separated from Violetzka's mouth. Tassie waited for his eyes to refocus.

'I'm afraid I have to go now,' she said.

'What?' It hadn't occurred to Billy she might leave.

'I'm goin'. Off. Offski. Home. You know.'

'But . . . but . . . what are we going to do? I mean, I was going to give you a reward or something! There's never been much in the money chest, but perhaps some land . . . or a house?'

'Oh,' said Tassie, thinking hard. 'Well, there is um, one thing I'd quite like . . . let me whisper . . .' Tassie, suddenly bashful, stood on tiptoe and muttered in his ear.

Billy's eyebrows shot up. And then he smiled and drew his ceremonial sword.

'You must kneel,' he commanded, borrowing his father's voice again. 'For your noble service to the House of Huffington in our time of utmost need, I, King William the First, proclaim you a Knight of the Realm. Arise, Sir Tassie of the Far Off Lands. You have won your spurs. Huffington salutes you!' And he struck her once on each shoulder with the flat of the blade. Tassie was pleased that he managed to miss both her ears and her jugular vein. It was perhaps the finest bit of swordsmanship he'd produced all day.

'That is just SO cool,' she said, really pleased. It didn't matter that she wouldn't be a knight once she got home, and none of her friends at school would ever believe her. Underneath, she'd always know that she had a title.

'Bye bye, Tassie,' said Violetzka, coming forward and kissing her on both cheeks before delivering a hug like an anaconda. 'You are ze true friend of Huffington and of Mazovia, and ze great mate also! Zank you so much. Ve shall be naming ze first childer for you! Vill you come visit at us?'

'I hope so,' said Tassie, meaning it. 'It sort of depends if I have the time.'

The shadows were beginning to lengthen as she caught up with her mother back in the castle courtyard. The Twins were hot and exhausted, and Lil looked like she was actually asleep, hanging from her mother's grasp.

'Thank goodness!' exclaimed Mrs Ripley when

Tassie appeared. 'We'll pick up your father on the way. Heaven knows where Gramma is. Didn't you have her last? Now, where did we leave the car? I wonder when the film will be out on DVD . . .?'

Tassie followed on behind her thinking it didn't seem too extraordinary that her parents hadn't realised they were in an entirely different century. Modern people didn't notice what was in front of their noses. As if to prove a point, they came across her father. He was standing outside the Banqueting Hall and gazing out over the scene around him.

'Of course, it's nothing like the *real* Middle Ages,' he said. 'Come on everyone. Let's go.'

The lights were on in the hall as the family trooped in together. Electric lights, Tassie noticed suddenly, as her insides did backflips. Her family all clutched their stomachs, looking confused. A great weight seemed to fall from her as the Balloon of Time finally got its own way and pinged out round and whole again, with everyone in their rightful century.

The police cars were still outside in the car park,

and their strobing lights circled the walls like a school disco, but there had been some tidying up since the Ripleys had fled the century. Pieces of broken furniture were piled neatly against the walls, ready for restoring. Tapestries had been rehung, and someone had tried to put the suits of armour back together without an instruction leaflet, so they looked like metal mutants.

Mr Ripley stopped over by the enormous fireplace, where the Spotty Guide was being led from the hall by two coppers.

'Oh well done, chaps!' he said happily. The Spotty Guide made a peculiar noise, and looked around for a weapon. 'Well, got to go!' said Mr Ripley, jingling his car keys carelessly. 'Thank you so much for a *lovely* day. It's been a lot of fun.'

And then suddenly, there was Gramma, all big skirts and lacy top. It was as if she'd never been a flighty young filly galloping the sporting fields of the thirteenth century with a furious appetite for oats. Tassie went up and hugged her, relieved to see the old lady again.

'Look,' said Gramma simply. She stood back and waved a pudgy arm at the vast wall at the back of the hall. The pictures still hung where they had been, but every single one had changed. Tassie gasped as she walked down the row. Young knights smiling. Ladies dressed in bright clothes with a merry spark in their eyes. Horses' heads held high with pride and spirit. Even the stern-looking matron with the big bosom was glancing flirtatiously over her shoulder.

'Wow!' breathed Tassie in wonder. 'It worked.'

'Didn't I tell you?' said Gramma, nodding with satisfaction. 'I knew if I told you what to do everything would be all right.'

Tassie was just opening her mouth indignantly when she came across the painting of Billy. He wasn't in armour any more, but in a rather fetching silk padded jacket and yellow tights that showed up his unwarrior-like knees. He looked older, sleek and happy, and his cornflower eyes still had the slightly spaced-out look of the incurable poet. Next to him, holding his hand adoringly was Violetzka, and cradled in her other arm was a baby, laughing up at them. Tassie looked quickly down at the plate on the frame. *King William I of Huffington, Queen Violetzka, and their first born – Prince Tassie, Duke of Mazovia.*

'Muppets,' giggled Tassie happily. 'Bet he'll get teased at school.'

As she turned away to follow her family and Gramma outside, her eye was caught by an enormous tapestry that she could swear hadn't been there earlier. On it was embroidered a scene of medieval life – a big carnival with knights and peasants, animals and acrobats. Looking closer, she was surprised to make out the enormous figure of the Black Baron, right in the centre. His arm was raised in the air, clutching a huge bunch of coloured ribbons that ran, like spokes of a wheel, to the hands of grubby peasant children. The children were skipping happily around this human Maypole. Looking closer still, Tassie could see in the ice-chip eyes of Sir Brutus of Badspite that he rather wished he'd been sent to the Crusades instead.

KATIE ROY

Katie Roy was brought up in the Chilterns, and fed on adventure books from a very early age. When she grew up she decided to have adventures of her own, so she did a lot of travelling. But that didn't quite feel adventurous enough, so she became a TV reporter for the British Forces Television, which really did the trick. Following British troops around the globe meant that she got into a lot of sticky situations, but they always got her out of them. After quite a few years of rebels and guns and wars, and helicopters and refugees, not to mention earthquakes and floods, Katie decided to try her hand at writing children's books. This turned out to be much harder than she'd ever expected but at least she didn't need to wear body armour or sleep in a ditch to do it!

COMING IN MARCH 2010 . . .

The Quest of the Warrior SHEEP

All is quiet on Eppingham Farm.
The sheep that live there chew cud and cauliflower.
Sometimes they butt fence posts.

Until one day a silvery object falls on their heads.
Sal, the Southdown Ewe,
knows their great Sheep God must be in danger.
'Only we can save him!' she cries.

And so the quest of the Warrior Sheep begins.

But who are the men in the yellow car
and why are they following?

The Warriors will need to hold on to their fleeces . . .

It's absolutely baaarmy!

EGMONT PRESS: ETHICAL PUBLISHING

Egmont Press is about turning writers into successful authors and children into passionate readers – producing books that enrich and entertain. As a responsible children's publisher, we go even further, considering the world in which our consumers are growing up.

Safety First
Naturally, all of our books meet legal safety requirements. But we go further than this; every book with play value is tested to the highest standards – if it fails, it's back to the drawing-board.

Made Fairly
We are working to ensure that the workers involved in our supply chain – the people that make our books – are treated with fairness and respect.

Responsible Forestry
We are committed to ensuring all our papers come from environmentally and socially responsible forest sources.

For more information, please visit our website at www.egmont.co.uk/ethical

Mixed Sources
Product group from well-managed forests and other controlled sources
www.fsc.org Cert no. TT-COC-002332
© 1996 Forest Stewardship Council

Egmont is passionate about helping to preserve the world's remaining ancient forests. We only use paper from legal and sustainable forest sources, so we know where every single tree comes from that goes into every paper that makes up every book.

This book is made from paper certified by the Forestry Stewardship Council (FSC), an organisation dedicated to promoting responsible management of forest resources. For more information on the FSC, please visit **www.fsc.org**. To learn more about Egmont's sustainable paper policy, please visit **www.egmont.co.uk/ethical**.

CL121139